solitude

and

Other Stories

THE RICHARD SULLIVAN PRIZE IN SHORT FICTION

Editors
William O'Rourke and Valerie Sayers

1996,   *Acid,* Edward Falco

1998,   *In the House of Blue Lights,* Susan Neville

2000,   *Revenge of Underwater Man,* Jarda Cervenka

2002,   *Do Not Forsake Me, Oh My Darling,*
          Maura Stanton

2004,   *Solitude and Other Stories,* Arturo Vivante

solitude

and

Other Stories

by

Arturo Vivante

University of Notre Dame Press
Notre Dame, Indiana

Copyright © 2004 by Arturo Vivante
Published by the University of Notre Dame Press
Notre Dame, Indiana 46556
www.undpress.nd.edu
All Rights Reserved

Manufactured in the United States of America

Library of Congress Cataloging-in-Publication Data
Vivante, Arturo.
Solitude, and other stories / by Arturo Vivante.
p.   cm. — (The Richard Sullivan prize in short fiction)
ISBN 0-268-04365-5 (alk. paper)
ISBN 0-268-04366-3 (pbk. : alk. paper)
1. New England—Social life and customs—Fiction.
2. Canada—Social life and customs—Fiction.   3. Italy—Social life
and customs—Fiction.   I. Title.   II. Series.
PS3572.I85S65   2004
813'.54—dc22

                                                    2004000743

∞ *This book is printed on acid-free paper.*

In memory of my wife

contents

Acknowledgments   ix

Honeymoon   1
The Foundling   9
Musico   23
Train Ride of a Faun   33
Shelter   37
The Cove   43
The Foghorn   59

The Park   63

To Mock the Years   71

Solitude   77

Dante   89

The Italian Class   97

Escapes   107

Can-Can   115

The Cricket   119

The Sugar Maples   125

Stones Aplenty   137

The Homing Pigeon   141

Company   149

Crosscurrents   159

Osage Orange   167

Reflection   179

Fall and Rise   185

Doves   195

contents

acknowledgments

Stories in *Solitude* have been published in the following journals:

"Honeymoon," "The Fog Horn," "The Park," and "Osage Orange," *New Yorker*

"The Foundling," *Bostonia*

"Musico," *Arts Review*

"Faun," *New York Times*

"Shelter," "The Italian Class," and "The Sugar Maples," *Yankee Magazine*

"The Cove," *TriQuarterly*

"To Mock the Years," *Sycamore Review*

"Solitude" and "The Cricket," *Notre Dame Review*

"Dante" and "Company," *Santa Monica Review*

"Escapes," *Antaeus*

"Can-Can," *London Magazine*

"The Homing Pigeon," *Salmagundi*

"Crosscurrents," *Shenandoah*

"Reflection," *Formations*

"Fall and Rise" and "Doves," *Cape Cod Voice*

solitude

and

Other Stories

honeymoon

Lying on a haystack, Girolamo picks a smooth golden straw—one that the rain hasn't blackened—and makes of it a ring around Fiorella's finger. He does the same in the field with a blade of grass, then stretches it vertical between his thumbs and blows on it, raising a silence-sundering sound. And in the woods he uses gorse. Always on Sundays. On weekdays, he works grazing his flock way up on the slopes of the mountain.

"When are you going to put a real ring around my finger?" she asks.

"Soon soon," he replies, and wonders. Her head is resting on his arm. They are both looking up at the sky. "Soon," he says again, wistfully.

He has to tend the sheep many more months before he will have sold enough wool, enough cheese, for the ring and the house. She, too, is working at it. She sews all day and knits evenings. She cuts. She embroiders on her cloth and her future. Her life is fleece-white; it is rose; it is golden. The pillowcases have her and Girolamo's initials entwined. She dreams of the house: the brick floor is waxed; the fireplace in the kitchen is lighted, the flames lick the crown and roots of a chestnut and shine on the brass of the firedogs; the water in the lidded black caldron over the flames is getting hotter and hotter. After supper, Girolamo will lift it off the hook and carry it to the sink for her. The sink is of stone—one huge slab, carved hollow and so smooth no grease will stick to it. The sheet she's hemming is one of a stack. They will smell good in the closet from lavender stems twisted back over the blossoms and tied in the shape of a spool.

Girolamo, too, has visions of what the house will be like. He sees heavy salamis hanging from rafters, hams well coated with pepper, festoons of sausages, drums of cheese oiled on the surface and aging. He wonders if he will have a car. To have one, the road must be improved. The big cobblestones are all right for mules and his donkey, but for a car he must get fine gravel. And the last stretch may be too steep, even in first gear.

The house isn't ready. So far, it isn't much more than a barn—a barn and a pen—on the rim of the hamlet, where the road ends and the paths start that he and the sheep have made. First thing to be built is a staircase. The loft of the barn must be floored, two inside walls put up, doors hung, and several windows. They will have a bathroom. The old people don't, but all newly-weds have them. These things he ponders as he grazes his sheep. Sometimes one strays from the fold. Then he picks up a stone and throws it so it will land beyond her and make her turn back. He can throw stones amazingly far. Last year, he had a dog he could trust. But Tosco died, and the new one isn't so smart. Sometimes he has to walk miles for one sheep, and it isn't fun at night, when you can hear the wolves howl. The women here don't call them wolves but refer to them as *bestiacce*—"bad beasts." As with cancer and hail, there is the feeling that naming isn't very far from invoking.

With the first frosts, the grass begins to wither, and the sheep spend more time in their pens or are taken to greener pastures. When he was a child, they took them down to graze in the lowlands by the sea, where the grass is green all year round. He used to follow the flock down the winding road to the valley, and down the valley all the way to the sea. The journey lasted three days. The flock looked like a cloud down the road, and there would be other flocks at short intervals before them and after. Sometimes in the sky rows of clouds would take the same route down the valley. He followed the sound of the sheep's bells, and often, stick in hand, he would have to drive them to one side to make room for a car. In recent years, the traffic has got so forbidding the shepherds truck their sheep down to their winter pastures or keep them here on the mountain and feed them hay and other fodder. That's what Girolamo does. He stays. He works on the house. He saws timber for rafters. He carries bricks up from a kiln in the plain, and because bricks are expensive he adds stones—beautiful square ones that he finds. He mixes cement, and carries pail after pail up the ladder. But the actual building is done by a mason.

The staircase is finished. It is an outside one, on the south side of the house. Before, to get to the second floor, there was just a ladder to a window. Fiorella will have geraniums in pots on the balustrade. She has half a dozen embroidered new sheets. They are thick, rough, made of coarse linen, and they'll wear a long time. She wonders when she and Girolamo will sleep between them. She'll wash them down at the hamlet's fountain, even if they are going to have running water.

There are many days in the winter when the weather is so bad you can't work outside. Still, each week some progress is made on the house.

The days lengthen. In March, the slopes of the mountain are threaded with green—new green, fresh over the seared blades of last year. In the house, the partitions are up and being plastered. There's a good smell of mortar about. New faces appear—an electrician, a plumber. The house is being wired, is being piped. Now for the finishing touches—the bathtub, the faucets, the bowl, in the kitchen the sink and the stove. Soon Lent will be over, and then . . .

The day comes. A wedding is always in season, but best in the spring. He has a ring for her—golden, just right. They bought it down at the village—ten miles from the hamlet—one Saturday morning. "A beautiful hand," the jeweler said, peering through his thick lenses close enough that his lips skimmed the slender fingers.

The bridegroom, in a blue suit and white tie, looks unfamiliar, so different from when in the fields, his clothes faded, the sweater made of the wool of his sheep. But he isn't self-conscious. He smiles; he seems full of energy, zest. The bride moves nimbly. The white dress she has made fits snug round her waist. As they walk away from the altar, she leans on him. They seem to be hurrying toward the future that beckons there beyond the door, which is open. At the wedding reception they are solicitous, full of attentions, and go around from one guest to the other, welcoming, toasting, inviting people to visit their home as soon as they get back from their honeymoon—an overnight excursion to Rome, where neither of them has been.

"Oh, we'll give you time to settle down; don't expect us for a week or two," a married friend says.

"A week or two? No, you be sure and come along before that! We like company."

"Company?" someone else says. "You don't need company now. You've got each other for that."

"I shouldn't want any other company, not for years—not if I had a warm, good little woman like that," an older guest says, with a glint in his eyes.

"You go slow, Grandpa, with that kind of talk," a relative says, and they laugh.

Fiorella and Girolamo are spirited, joyful all through the party.

But on the train to Rome they sit self-conscious in the compartment; they hold hands; they stick close together and talk only in whispers. His face is flushed. His tie seems to constrict him. His jacket is buttoned up. And she hardly ever looks around her—she looks down at her hands or at him. In front of them, a paunchy middle-aged man is reading the paper. His wife sits erect, stern, disapproving. Of what? There are two tourists—a young man and a girl, in khaki shorts and gray sweatshirts, their haversacks on the racks and a washed-out look on their faces.

In Rome, the hotel—the first one either of them ever has been to—recommended by a friend is old, small, near the station. She looks at the sheets—sleazy, so thin they are almost transparent, and questionably clean. She touches the radiator, which is warm, though it is April. At the hamlet, even in winter they'll have no heat in their bedroom. To warm the bed, after supper she'll put some live cinders from the kitchen hearth into an open pan, cover them with ashes, and hang it from a wooden sledlike framework that she'll slide in between the sheets. It is a luxury that even the poorest of the poor can afford and won't do without.

The hotel room is meager, but never mind—for dinner they'll go to a world-famous place: Alfredo's.

They sit side by side. At a table opposite theirs, by the wall, another couple is sitting, about their age. She is a striking brunette in a green taffeta dress. Her eyebrows, the curve of her cheeks and mold of her chin seem to have been carved in one felicitous stroke. She is perfectly at ease. And she assumes poses you don't see up on the mountain. As the young man talks to her, she laughs, once or twice holding on to his forearm. He has a bright look about him; his face lights up when he speaks; he is spare, thin-nosed, tawny-haired, and apparently very entertaining. He's fussy about the wine. He knows just what to order.

Girolamo and Fiorella, on the other hand, are hardly conversing. They often gaze or catch each other gazing across the tables at the couple opposite. The recipients of their attention don't seem to mind. One passing look is all that comes from them. They say a few words to each other, and a knowing smile rests briefly on their faces.

At last, dinner is over. Fiorella and Girolamo go back to their hotel. At last, they are in bed. Sleep should follow love, but it doesn't. She is thinking of the girl in the restaurant, and the way Girolamo looked at her. He probably wishes he were married to her. Up in the hamlet and for miles around, she is the prettiest, but down here where does she stand? She's nothing. Her looks are lost on this city.

He can't sleep, either. He still sees his wife looking at the tawny-haired, smart-looking young man. He is certain she wishes *he* were her husband. And why shouldn't she? What is he, anyway? A poor shepherd, ignorant of the ways of the world.

"Tell me the truth," she says in a whisper. "Do you wish I were that girl who was sitting opposite us at Alfredo's?"

"No, why?"

"You kept looking at her."

"Silly, I wasn't looking at her," Girolamo says. "I was looking at him, thinking you liked him better than me. You had your eyes on him, I know."

"But I didn't!" says Fiorella. "*She* was the one I was looking at, thinking you wished you were married to her."

"And I thought—"

"So did I!"

They laugh. They hug each other. Sleep this time follows love.

They wake at six, the time they usually rise. They can hear the hum of the city. On the mountain, even at noon, everything is so still that if you see a man chopping wood across the valley you can hear the sharp blows distinctly seconds after they fall. That is, if the wind doesn't drown them. It can howl for weeks without pause, till the whole mountain seems to be shrieking, for the hamlet is near the divide—this side the rivers flow into the Tyrrhenian Sea, the other side into the Adriatic. Now, why would they want to live there? From down here the hamlet seems endlessly high—way up, near the stars, itself a constellation at night, and in the daytime a few rocks put together out of the numberless rocks of the mountain. Is it really there? He thinks of his sheep; he knows each of them one from the other, and he reviews them. It's a good way of knowing that they are true. He couldn't possibly invent them. And the house is true, and the stones of the mountain. And the wind is true, and the cries of the wolves.

After breakfast, they visit the Colosseum and St. Peter's. In the afternoon, they have to decide which of two trains to take home. "Shall we take the early one?" he asks.

"Yes," she replies.

Soon the mountains appear in the distance, chain after chain. Somewhere in that misty blue a white speck is their hamlet, and new and ready is a house waiting for them; in it a table is laden with gifts, and a bed is made. The pillowcases have their initials embroidered; the covers are folded. They have only to slip in. No—there's still a long way to go. But the train rushes on.

honeymoon

the foundling

The sculptor was called Gemito. A self-given
name. It means "wail" in Italian. And he called and
signed himself that because he had been found, a
wailing newborn, by the front door of a church in
Naples, early one summer morning in the middle
of the last century. Who had left him there? A
young mother most likely. He never knew. Never
knew her or his father or who they were. A pass-
erby, alerted by the wailing, climbed up the church
steps to the door and found him, and took him to
the carabinieri, bearing him like a gift.

They made an inquiry. He was written up in the newspapers. But no one claimed the infant; no one was able to trace who had left him there or his origins. He was taken to a hospital and reared in the children's ward, then given to an orphanage.

At the elementary school, to which the orphanage children were led each morning in a group dressed in gray uniforms, his teacher soon found he had an extraordinary gift for drawing. His weren't stick figures like most children's, but curved and full-bodied. He drew his teacher and classmates, catching their likeness in a few bold strokes. "Do me, do me!" the children would shout and mill around to see the result.

After a few years of school he was apprenticed to a carpenter in exchange for food and lodging. Many of his early drawings, and later, a bust entitled *The Philosopher*, depict that carpenter—a bright, bearded man. When Gemito was nine he worked as a delivery boy for a tailor, one of whose clients was a sculptor. He became the young boy's first art teacher, but before long, ever impatient, Gemito left him, and two years later showed a folder of his drawings to another sculptor who put him to work on a statue of Brutus. But the strict adherence to academic principles that the sculptor demanded left little room for freedom of expression, and he quit this master too.

Next he worked in a pottery. He went to Vietri, the pottery town down the coast, where clay seemed to blossom and fructify. As he modeled and molded the clay, and as the clay took shape in his hands, he felt it also taking the shape of his thoughts—and he felt himself thinking in clay. His teachers now were the ancient sculptors who had fashioned the bronzes unearthed at Pompeii, and the seething vibrant life all around him in Naples. He had to reconcile the two sources of his inspiration—the classic and the picturesque—and come upon something new, something fresh and his own. He had to get away from the formalized and the formal, and find form in the informal, in the flux of the past and the present. To his wonder he could sell his art. It was in demand. At first, unsigned, to carpenters, architects, decorators, jewellers—to anyone who needed an ornament; but later on, figures he signed, figures that accompanied nothing and stood on their own. He divined the spirit of the times, played hide-and-seek with it, and was more often ahead of it than behind it. He knew what was needed, knew what went and what didn't, but he made no compromises with truth or truth as he saw it. While still in his teens he prepared and exhibited a series of terra-cotta heads, most remarkable among them that of a sick child. The show had an enormous success. Eighteen years after he was born, his name again appeared in the papers.

He was commissioned to do all sorts of portraits, many of celebrities, like Verdi and Amedeo of Savoy, but he was at his best doing figures of his own people: a water boy, a little fisher boy and a Gypsy woman. His work was acclaimed, even in Paris, and he prospered. But his joy was in the doing; in the fervor of his work he quite forgot himself and was ecstatic. Once a piece was done, he fell into a disconsolate state. Dissatisfaction, that bugbear of artists, assailed him. He felt listless, dispirited, sullen. Gone was grace; he was in the throes of despair and dejection. Dejection has this jolly feature: it deprives you even of the will to help yourself, and he lay in his studio, now face down, now staring at the ceiling. Then unexpectedly, perhaps from the blankness of that very ceiling, a figure seemed to emerge, an idea came to his rescue, and with the idea energy, and he would stir, spring back to life.

He was very conscious of being a foundling and he often wondered who his parents might have been. In that bustling city he gazed at the streetwalkers. Perhaps one of them was his mother, older now, not a girl any longer, and since he didn't have one in particular to love, he loved them all. But in a different way from his friends. His was a deep, secret attachment. And his father, who was he? He could have been anyone. Perhaps a sailor from far away. The possibilities were immense. He loved the whole world. And sometimes he hated it, too, for having abandoned him there by that church that he so often went to visit, and for the circumstances that had led his mother to leave him. Oh, he could hardly blame her, he blamed the injustices that were at the root of her action, the unequal struggle, the shame, the shame and the guilt that people had made her feel. As he grew older he read about Moses and Oedipus, and he identified with both. He knew by heart the lines in which Oedipus says:

> I am not ashamed of my origin, no matter how humble it may be.
> I am fortune's child and glad to be no other than myself.

And the chorus saying:

> Was a woodland nymph your mother, loved by Pan upon the hills?
> Or was it Apollo that she lay with on a fresh green grassy hollow? Was it Hermes on the hills? Was it Bacchus by the springs?

No, the truth was probably more bitter; perhaps he was conceived in a brothel where sore need and lust, not love, had begot him. Perhaps it was in a hovel, and incest was at his origin. He would impulsively rid himself of these ugly thoughts. It was love, it was hot-blooded passion that made him! A girl, a virgin with her first love—a boy not much older than herself—had made him, or else a man she couldn't possibly marry, and in his mind he retraced her pains again and again, and the insult and terror, and her labor. Whoever he, Gemito, was, he was almost certainly born out of wedlock. A bastard then; he hated the word. "Illegitimate"—he hated that word even more.

He had his world to find comfort in, his art, the clay that he molded, the marble, the wood that he carved. Often it was children he made, or youths, or young women. They were his family. He needed no other. Art was kinder than life. Life had so much that art could do without. Art could dispense with the weight that oppressed him. Compared to life, art was as light as a shadow. In his art he could choose whatever he wanted. There were no limits, no bounds. He was free, as free as his dancers, as free as his Cupid and as swift as the arrow of his bow, as happy as Narcissus admiring himself in a pool, as winged as angels, as strong as Samson, as wily as Delilah. What else, who else did he need? Nothing and no one. He was himself, self-made, without antecedents. No one to feel thankful or indebted to. Self-sustaining and self-sufficient. Everyone's son and no one's.

For a time he lived in Rome. The air of the city seemed conducive to greatness. Here there were humbling sights. It was like a sea of time. He liked especially the Capitoline building, each of whose floors belonged to a different age, and the Palatine where he could wander in peace. The arches, the gardens, the churches, the fountains inspired him. Show followed show. The critics took serious note of his work. He was commissioned to do more and more. Soon not merely the galleries, but museums asked for his work, and not only in Rome. He was famous.

And yet he still had something of the foundling about him, the street urchin. He possessed a disarming simplicity, almost a nakedness. He felt uncomfortable in a tie, jacket or anything formal. He wore his old, loose working clothes and went about open-collared, often in corduroys. Oh, one good brown suit he had, but he hardly ever wore it, except at funerals and occasional receptions.

The king commissioned him to do a silver service, and when it was delivered invited him to court to have dinner at the Quirinal.

"Oh, Gemito," a friend said to him, "you have to wear tails."

"But I have no such thing."

"Then buy them."

"No, I am a child of the people. They don't wear tails. I wouldn't feel right in them."

"But you must. They all do at court, unless you are in the military and wear a uniform. Tails are *de rigueur,* or at least a dinner jacket."

"No," he said and brooded over the matter. He brooded over it for days, unwilling to change his ways or his attire, not even for a king. A week passed and he did nothing about it. He was supposed to have dinner at the Quirinal the next day.

"What are you going to do?"

"I don't know."

"If you don't want to buy one, I'll lend you mine," a friend said.

"No, I despise tails. I won't wear them. I am an artist; they'll have to take me as I am."

"They won't let you in."

"Oh yes they will. The dinner party is for me."

"Don't fool yourself, there'll be plenty of others."

"I don't care. Let them do as they like, and I will too."

He lived and worked on Via Margutta. There he took his good brown suit out of a closet, went out to buy a bottle of black dye, and in his studio he poured it into a cauldron of boiling water. He soaked it in the cauldron. Then, he hung it up to dry. The next day, in the evening, he had it pressed. "It's still a little humid," the woman who had pressed it said to him, "but it will keep the crease better this way."

"But I'm wearing it tonight."

"Tonight? I'd better press it again."

"Never mind, there's no time. I have to go now. I'll put it on and it'll dry on me, with my body heat."

At the Quirinal, the guards—the *corazzieri,* hand-picked men who stood well over six feet, looked him over suspiciously, but the majordomo, who knew exactly who everyone was, came out to welcome him. There were many other guests—ladies in evening gowns and men in white ties and tails—but he wasn't self-conscious; he wasn't one to be intimidated. He had plenty to say without having to resort to any of the numerous conversation pieces around. At table he was seated next to the queen in a huge chair upholstered in red velvet. Everyone congratulated him on the silver service. "Here's to a new Benvenuto Cellini," somebody said, and they toasted. He talked about how he had wrought it. It was his night. If anyone possessed an aura it was he. But when dinner was over and he finally got up from his chair, there on the red velvet was the black imprint of his suit. The king didn't notice, but the queen did and frowned. He explained. They laughed. Even the queen tried to laugh. Someone patted him on the shoulder then checked his hand. It all added to his fame, the incident even making *Marcaurclio,* the Italian equivalent of *Punch.* But he was never invited back.

"So how's the food at the king's?" the owner of the *Antico Botaro,* the trattoria he went to every night with friends and models, asked him.

"You want to know? It's better here."

He was thirty-five, and at the height of his fame. He went back to Naples to work on a statue of Charles V for the royal palace there. But what did he have to do with kings and emperors, he asked himself. He felt he had to rid himself of his worldly, mundane traits and renew himself by seeking loneliness. The inner turmoil that had never left him now presented itself in a much fiercer way. No, it was worse than that: he feared he would lose his mind, and like a wounded thing he felt an urge to hide in order to heal. He found a small room and for over twenty years he lived there like a hermit. In his self-confinement he could hardly sculpt, but drawing required so little in the way of materials. And what was subtler and more knowing than the fine, pure line of a pencil? What secrets might it not uncover? His draftsmanship grew from this period, and never ceased to develop. He achieved greater and greater refinement.

Slowly he recovered and reappeared in public. He bought a beautiful house. Downstairs was his studio, upstairs his living quarters. He continued drawing. In sculpture he found silver and gold more responsive than bronze. He did a self-portrait: a drawing of a furrow-browed man with searching eyes, long wavy white hair down to his shoulders and equally wavy long beard and mustache, like Leonardo. He is wearing a checked shirt, and his right arm crosses the paper in the act of drawing.

He must have been quite a striking figure walking the streets of Naples. He became attuned to the city, its color, its warmth. He made new friends and old friends came to visit. Once an ascetic, he became an epicurean. The models returned. On streets and squares he was continuously greeted. Yes, he felt very much at home here on the streets, so much at home that at times he felt there were no strangers and that the whole population of Naples was his family. This was, he thought, the most theatrical of cities. Scene after scene after scene. How could one tire of it? How could one be lonely here where all kinds of people bowed to him, took off their hats, said hello, hugged him, kissed him? Though he often went to the theater and to the opera, he sometimes felt that he didn't need to go: out on the street you could hear workmen and women singing. Their voices reached him from parted windows and courtyards; the alleys rang with them. The theater, the opera were right here—out in the open.

He still walked to the church where he had been found. There he would pause to look at the steps and the huge door, then resume walking, and he would sink deep in thought wondering who his mother and father might have been. Perhaps someone right in this neighborhood, still alive though very old, and he looked at those much older than himself with inquiring, sympathetic eyes.

Returning home he sometimes felt lonely, as he never felt away from it. Lonely not for a wife and children—art was his wife, he thought, and his children were his statues—but for a mother and a father. One day when he went out, a very old beggar woman asked him for a coin. He readily gave it to her and wondered if she could be his mother. He followed her and caught up with her. Not realizing that he was the same man who had just given her a coin, she stretched out her hand. He gave her another, and then he asked, "Where do you live?"

"Eh, where do I live? I live where I can. Here and there. We are the poor."

"Don't you have a bed?"

"A bed? I have no bed. Rags I sleep on, back of an old shed, near the railroad. In the winter, when it's cold, there's a grotto. It's warmer underground."

"Show me."

"Eh, show me," she mocked him with a gesture of annoyance. "And what do you want? What d'you want from me?"

"Nothing."

"Ah good, because I've got nothing. Nothing's all I have. Old age, that's what I have. I am older than you, and I look even older than I am."

Could this old woman be his mother? She was the right age—fifteen, twenty years older than he was. Yet the chances were almost nil. "And you have no family, no husband, no children?"

"None. I'm all alone."

"You've never had any children?"

"I never had anybody."

"But when you were young—you must have been young—what did you do?"

"What did I do when I was young? I walked. I walked the streets as I do now, but then people turned to look and I could make more money."

"And you've lost it all."

"I never saved it. There was never much to save."

"I have a house," he said, "a large house, and some spare rooms, comfortable rooms, warm, with beds, furniture and carpets. Would you like to come and live there?"

She looked at him as if he were crazy.

"I mean it," he said.

She still looked at him the same way, without saying a word.

He took his wallet out of his pocket and gave her a bank note and a card with his name and address on it. She looked at the crisp bank note avidly, fingered it and stuffed it in her apron pocket under a bedraggled shawl, then glanced at the card. "I can't read or write," she said.

He told her his address. "Come if you want to," he said, and left her staring at him.

There was never a dearth of beggars in Naples. As he walked toward his home he was soon approached by another beggar, this one an old man. That one too could be his parent, he thought; the man looked old enough to be his father. He gave him a silver coin.

"Thank you and God bless you," the old man said and clasped the hand that had given it with both of his, moaned and brought it to his lips and kissed it.

"Where do you live?" he asked him.

"Down by the docks."

"And do you have a bed to sleep on?"

"No, I don't have one. We sleep on the floor."

"Who's we?"

"The likes of me. Beggars. Where else can we sleep?"

"And is there any sort of shelter?"

"There's shelter from the rain, but not from the wind."

"And did you ever have a family?"

"I had a family when I was a kid, but they put me out. Too many mouths to feed."

"And a wife and children?"

"No, I never could afford it. Unemployed most of my life I've been. I was a fisherman for a time, then the weather got me." The man was all hunched over.

"I have a house, a good house."

"I am sure you do, a man like you."

"Would you like to come and live there?"

The old man stared at him as the old woman had done.

"Would you? It's warm and comfortable and there's a bed, and food."

"A bed, food, what wouldn't I do for a bed and food?"

"Then come." Again he took his wallet out, gave him a bank note and his card.

"I can't read at my age," he said. "I have no reading glasses."

He told him where he lived. "Come if you like," he said, and left him there.

The next day, at different times, both beggars appeared at his doorstep and they were let in by his maid, whom he had alerted of their possible visit. They were each led to a separate bedroom and fed. Then they were fitted out with clothes, for the man had brought nothing and the woman only a small bundle in a kerchief whose corners she had tied into a knot.

To his friends Gemito said he had adopted a father and a mother. And this eccentricity too increased his fame as an original.

They lived quietly, the two ex-beggars, in their good rooms. They took their meals with him. The woman helped the maid cook, and the man dried the dishes. Much of the day they were out walking the streets and, as old habits persist, they had trouble getting used to not stretching their hands out for coins. He gave each an allowance, as to a child. Both of them showed an inordinate interest in money, but he was a generous man and he increased their allowance from time to time. Possessions too, which they'd never had, they seemed to crave, and he gave them little presents, and sometimes not so little. Deep into their pockets the things would go, as into a vault. The woman, it turned out, had a good ear for music, knew a lot of old Neapolitan songs, was in fact a veritable treasure trove of them. On and on and on she would sing, one song after another, in a thin reedy voice that never failed.

No, they weren't his mother and father. That had been only a fancy. But he clung to that fancy. Its brightness didn't diminish. And he was glad of what he had done; it brought a degree of humor to his mind and conversation. He would proudly present his "mother" and "father" to his friends. "How are your folks?" they would ask with a knowing smile, and he would smile back just as knowingly. He did portraits of them in pen and ink and in clay. One of them he called *The Penates,* for at times they seemed to him ageless as household gods. They were given birthday presents and name-day presents, and presents for the day they came to stay, which was to them like a second birth. And they gave presents to Gemito, for his birthday and his name day (St. Vincent's)—though everyone called him Gemito, his first name was Vincenzo. The woman gave him a sweater she knit for him, the man a little wooden sailboat he carved. Anything at all in the household was an excuse or occasion for dinner parties and toasts, music and songs. It was as if he had to make up for the years of solitude with company and cheer.

But the two old people did have that peculiar greed, and, what was most extraordinary, he noticed that when he walked with them they resented his giving any handouts to the poor or to charities. It was as if they had a vested interest in his holdings and feared that his generosity with the dispossessed might cut into their share of the inheritance, in case—God forbid—they should survive him. It was ironic all right, though he was usually more amused than annoyed. Even so, once in a while, this greed of theirs got to him and they argued.

They didn't survive him, as was to be expected; in a few years they died, one soon after the other, and despite their defects, he missed them. He lived to be seventy-seven, becoming so prodigal in his old age that beggars would follow him on the street.

And when he died, there was a great crowd at his funeral—rich and poor, royalty and paupers. For a moment it was as if the brotherhood of man—the brotherhood he envisioned—had really come to pass.

musico

*I*n Rome a conductor used to be a neighbor of mine. He had a top-floor apartment with a fine view of the city, and a beautiful wife. I lived alone in a small second-floor apartment in the building next door. I can't remember how I met them. I was a doctor then. Perhaps he was a patient of mine. He has become very famous since. In those days he was just very well known, not famous, not famous worldwide anyway, and he, his wife, and I would sometimes go out and have dinner together.

"I've discovered a nice restaurant," I said one day. "Guido's. Do you want to go there?"

"Do they let itinerant musicians in?" he said.

"I don't know. None came when I was there. Why?"

"I can't stand them. Well, let's try it, but I warn you—"

"What'll you do if one of them comes in?"

"If one comes in, I go out. No, I've got a better idea. I'll warn the waiter."

We walked to Guido's and found a good table. He talked to the waiter about musicians, as he said he would.

"*Stia tranquillo, ci penso io*—don't worry. I'll see to it," the waiter said.

At a table near us was an old couple. Both had wedding rings on and a good part of the time they held hands, resting them on the white tablecloth.

Soon a musico did come in, a little old man, hesitantly, with a violin. The conductor glared at him, then at the waiter who immediately ushered him out. No doubt his being a conductor had something to do with that summoning look and the instant response he was able to elicit. As for me, I have the hardest time beckoning waiters.

"Why are you so against these itinerant players?" I said.

"Their music, or what they call music. They grind, they don't play, and it grates in my ear. I literally can't eat."

"He might have been an exception."

We went on with our meal, but I kept thinking of the old man who had been turned away. I don't know how long my reverie lasted—perhaps only a few minutes—but in it I saw a little apartment so poor and so shabby I wondered why it didn't look dreary. There was even a certain dignity about it. Was it because of the books and the piano? They lent an artistic touch, as if gentle winds were blowing through the windows and the room partook of the rose-violet light of late evening outside. It was shortly after sunset, and the rose and the violet were quickly fading outside. Inside, an elderly woman, graying, with the delicate, frail look of one who has suffered, rather pale, with pouting mouth and lips that were almost too soft but still had a touch of beauty and were like the fire of a smoldering charcoal resisting time under the veil of its ashes, was sitting by a table, embroidering linen. There was a pile of plain pieces of cloth on one side of her and a smaller pile on the other, representing the work of her day.

Her husband was at the piano, at his side a table with papers and musical scores. He played a few notes; after some silence he played again. From time to time he leaned over to write a note. He had a gaunt, slender figure and a dazed look, as if he lived in the light of his thoughts, not in the living room at all. He was wholly absorbed in his music when his wife missed a stitch.

"Here I go again missing a stitch," she said with impatience. "I can't see straight anymore; I can't go on. . . ." She paused a moment, looked at her cloth, then angrily threw it down. "And you do nothing to help." Her husband didn't take any notice of her, as though they had gone through the argument many times before. "Why? Why can't you do what I said?" she added.

He finally looked at her. "I can't do what you ask me to do," he replied. "I can't go and play the violin for a nickel in front of people who don't even listen."

"Pride, pride—that's all it is; and in the meantime we starve."

"We are not starving."

"Close to it. Old bread, market discards . . . I've been working all day, sewing till my eyes go blind. And what do you do? Tinker and fiddle around, arranging notes that won't go."

"You liked my music once."

"Once, once. You were all right as long as you played the violin. There were concerts; there were reviews in the papers; the whole orchestra liked you. But then playing wasn't creative enough—you had to go and start writing your own compositions."

"You used to encourage me then."

"We were young. The stars were smiling then; they twinkled brightly; they still twinkle—look at them twinkle through the skylight up there—but not for us anymore. If I try to look at them now the way I used to look at them then, tears rise at my lashes and all I see are tremulous streaks."

"You'd have more reason to cry if I cheapened myself and my music by playing in restaurants while people are gulping their food."

"What do you care if they listen or not?"

"Phonographs and jukeboxes don't care. But I do."

"But maybe someone would listen and appreciate what you play. In front of him maybe you'd play one of your original pieces. That person might be a conductor or a well-known impresario, have your symphonies published, all of your work sold and performed."

"You are more of a dreamer than I am."

"You don't even try. You hate to mix with the world. The farthest you've ever gone is the post office. You won't meet the important people, the people who count."

"Everyone counts."

"I mean those who could help you if you gave them a chance. You despise them. You say that they snub you, but I think it's you who snubs them."

"I've got to do things in my way. I can't change."

"To please me."

"I'll work washing dishes if it's money you want. I'll sweep the streets, be a waiter, carry big loads, rather than do what you ask me."

"As if you hadn't tried that already. And don't you remember what happened? They fired you after less than an hour. Look at you—who's going to hire you? Carry big loads! You are weak; you are an old man. At anything else than at music you are clumsy. But in music you are nimble."

"I am out of practice. You know that. All these years of composing . . . My fingers aren't as deft as my mind. The orchestras have all refused me."

"But people in restaurants are not so demanding. It won't be as at the concerts. If you slip a note, who will mind? And in the morning the dissonant note won't have an echo in the paper."

There was a long silence. For a few minutes one could hear only the hum of the city. Then he suddenly rose from his chair. "Where is my violin?" he said.

"Then you'll go?"

"Yes, what time is it?"

"Eight. A little past. Just the right time. The violin is out here. I'll get it."

Quickly, afraid he might change his mind, she went and got the violin from a closet. She handed it to him delicately.

He took it, looked at it for a long moment, and said, "I never thought I would prostitute you."

"It'll be only for a little while, you'll see; only for a little while."

He walked slowly toward the door.

"Shall I come with you? I could do the collecting."

"No, stay here. I don't think I could stand it if you came along."

He left, a haggard little figure of a man, and she watched him go, as if she would detain him. Slowly she closed the door but didn't leave it. She leaned against it, her forearm over her forehead. For a moment she stayed in that position, then crossed over to the window and looked for him on the busy street. She leaned out till she saw him, then followed him with her eyes till he disappeared around the corner. She returned to her chair, but she couldn't sew anymore. She went over to the bed and knelt on the floor, hiding her face in her arms. But she couldn't stay long in any position. A shadow descended on the room as, to save electricity, she switched the light off from over the piano.

musico

27

Hours passed, and from time to time, in the faint gloom of one lamp, she wandered about the room in distraction. More than once, in her anxiety over his not returning, she seemed about to leave the house and go searching for him in every restaurant. Several times she approached the door, opened it, and seemed undecided. The door opened into a dark rectangular space—the unlighted staircase. It suggested the unknown; it had something forbidding that advised her to remain where she was and wait. So, each time, she returned and crossed the room to the window, where she leaned out to scan the street, which now was quite deserted. Every once in a while she heard voices, and she started at the sound of each voice that she heard. Then, tired, she went and sat by the pile of linen, but she couldn't work.

At last she heard a little noise by the door and rushed to open it. It was only her cat, or rather not her cat but one of the city's stray cats with whom she had made friends and who came to visit her nearly every day, sometimes two or three times a day, sometimes not for a week. "Oh, it's you," she said. She picked it up and brought it over to her bed, where she sat, stroking it while it purred. "You didn't see him, did you? Have you come to tell me he isn't going to come back? What are you thinking? That it's high time I gave you some milk?"

She went into the kitchen and poured a little milk into a saucer. The cat followed her. "Why did I send him out? Tell me. Why did I let him go? It's late. Isn't he going to come back? Do you think he was in an accident? If only we had a phone. Has he left me forever? What do you think? Did I tell him he was no good? What did I tell him? I didn't mean it, whatever I said. It's me who's no good. Perhaps he went down to the Tiber. Did I tell him he was a failure? Oh, no, he didn't go down to the Tiber. No, no, soon I know he'll be here. Won't he?"

The cat looked at her only when he had finished his milk. "Maybe," she continued, "he'll come back with a bagful of coins, as silver as fish, and he'll drop them all on the floor to scatter like fish, roll to every corner of the room. I'll pick up every one, and we'll buy all sorts of things with them—things that we need and things we don't need; extravagant things we will buy. And we'll get the piano repaired. . . ."

She poured the cat a little more milk. "He didn't get drunk, did he? He didn't go and get drunk with that money? Is he sitting in a tavern or on the steps of some church, muttering to himself, saying: 'She wants me to play for a living, but I want to live so I can play.' He drank it, that money. It went into wine. He drank it to the last drop, so he could forget all about it."

The cat followed her into the living room, where she looked at a clock. It was nearly midnight. In a few minutes a distant church bell and then another tolled the hours. The cat brushed around her ankles. "Perhaps he's calling at several places because they give him so little and he wants to bring back a good sum. Restaurants stay open late. He plays them his music. They want to hear Neapolitan songs; they want to hear of Sorrento. But he knows no songs of Sorrento. He plays them pieces of Bach and Beethoven, his favorite tunes from Scarlatti. Do they listen? Some of them listen, and look at the violin dreamy-eyed. The music carries them far, far away." She herself seemed to hear it, saw an old married couple beckoning to him from their table, asking him to play them a waltz—the waltz that had introduced them—and humming it for him. Oh, such a sentimental old couple. She could see him listening to the tune for a moment, smiling a little, then playing. He played and composed as he played, something new, which followed their tune two or three seconds, then strayed into something his own, something unheard and unheard of. With the sound of that tune in his ears he rushed out. He went to the telegraph office—the only place he could find equipped with pencil and paper—and on a telegraph form he wrote the notes out. "Telegraph forms," she heard him

musico

saying, "they'll do for score sheets. Listen. I think it is a good composition, the best I've done in a long time."

"And the restaurant? You didn't go back?"

"It closed," he said with a curious smile. "I must have spent more time than I meant to out there in the telegraph office."

"It isn't true. Tell me the truth. It's too late in the night to tell stories."

"All right, I'll tell you what happened—I know that you like happy endings. That married old couple was moved to tears—have you ever heard of anyone so sentimental? They whispered something to each other, and then, looking at me with bright eyes, they invited me home. In a taxi we flew through the city. At their house I repeated the tune. They never seemed to tire of that music. Then they gave me this check for a present. Under the night sky and the stars I slowly made my way here; I seemed to be walking the heavens."

Now, she thought, he's coming up the steps. In a moment I'll hear the door being unlocked. She waited. Long she waited, then stepped toward the bed, lay down, and fell asleep.

Finally, a great while later, the door was unlocked and he entered. He had the sad expression of reality about him—no curious smile, no mysterious impressions. Silently, so as not to wake her, he went close to her. Tenderly, gently, he took a blanket and placed it over her and tucked her in, then, sitting on a chair, he started undressing, first taking one shoe off and then the other, which fell from his hand. She woke. "You are back," she said. "I am sorry I made you go."

"It wasn't so bad, not as bad as I thought it would be. Or only at the first place I went to. There a man glared at me, and, before I even started playing, he had the waiter turn me out."

"You are very quiet tonight," the conductor's wife said to me. "What are you thinking of?"

"What? Oh, nothing," I said. "I was just thinking of that man, that musico."

"Oh, him," the conductor said, and I told them briefly what I had imagined.

"Are you trying to make me feel guilty?" he said.

"It might not be the worst thing for you," she said.

"Well, it won't wash. You are much too romantic, not enough of a realist. That man ought to be husking corn."

train ride of a faun

What one is apt to discover in Italy is not necessarily what is new. Just as often, it can be something old, or even something primeval, as I have lately found.

On the single-track railroad line to Siena, the train seems to part its way through lush vegetation. Reeds and stray branches thrash the windows and wave as the train passes. And the smell of new-mown hay, broom and acacia blossoms, all in quick succession, enters in. Then, as we pull out of a small station, something even more surprising—a bare-foot youth appears wearing a sheepskin over his shoulders. Strange and yet familiar.

Looking at him, I am reminded of D. H. Lawrence saying that Italy is the one country where one can still meet a faun. This one doesn't have pointed ears or horns or hoofs or a goat's tail, but he suggests the peculiar things he has not. He stands by the door and looks about him warily, looks to this side and to that, uneasily. Then he comes forward hesitantly, like a creature of the woods entering open country. He proceeds down the aisle slowly and treads the floor so softly he seems to be walking on moss instead of linoleum. He finds a seat, but sits on the edge, as if it wasn't his due.

Soon, the conductor comes. Punch in hand, he strolls down the aisle and looks for new faces. He stops by the newcomer and asks for his ticket.

The youth looks back vacantly, a little bewildered.

"What? No ticket? Where are you going?"

"Castellina."

The conductor looks at his book of fares. His index finger turns several pages, runs down several lines, then stops. He names the price of the ticket, but there's no response. "You must get a ticket. Don't you know you can't travel without one?" Getting no answer, he concludes, "No ticket, out the next stop—Castellina."

"That's where I'm going," the youth says in a Tuscan accent.

The conductor shakes his head; his sagging figure sags more and he turns toward four elderly men in dark suits and collarless shirts who with grave attention have followed the proceedings from their seats nearby. "Ah," he sighs. "What can you do with people like that? Stop the train? They are not worth it. Send 'em to jail? You'd be doing them a favor. Woodsmen. Uncivilized woodsmen."

At that moment, a strange music superimposes itself on the noise of the wheels, and I see that the "uncivilized woodsman" is playing a shepherd's flute. The music gains the whole car. The conductor himself turns and pauses, and listens. The music rises above the sound of the train, and falls back on it, as into more than silence. It is no popular tune, no well-known aria, but sounds like something altogether unlearned, his very own. And as I look at him I think of the subtle figures on Etruscan vases, and of the Grecian Urn. He seems to be playing not to us but to a flock of goats (and hoping perhaps for a nymph to overhear him).

Near Castellina, as the train begins to slow down, so does his melody wane, and he rises, tucks the rough-hewn flute into his pocket and leaves, taking quick strides, as if he wanted no more of our stuffy world.

shelter

Years ago when I was a college student in Montreal, there used to be (and perhaps there still is) off a trail on one of the highest ridges of the Laurentian Mountains of Quebec, a log cabin, built, I think, by the province, or possibly by lumber-jacks, for people to take shelter in during storms and blizzards. It was a simple, windowless structure with an unlocked door, a wooden bunk, a shelf, and a rudimentary fireplace made of rocks. I stopped there with some friends during a cross-country skiing tour. We lit a fire, made some coffee, then went on to a lodge in a village down in the valley.

In the months that followed, I often thought of the cabin, remote and vacant up there in the mountains, and one weekend in late October I went to the village again, alone this time, meaning to retrace the trail we had taken through the woods. Beautiful as they had been in the winter, the woods would be even more beautiful now in autumn.

I had a knapsnack with a good blanket, some food, and a flashlight, and rather than stay at the lodge, which I could hardly afford, I decided to climb the mountain and look for the log cabin on the ridge.

It was evening, the air crisp, invigorating. A few clouds in the west matched the crimson of the leaves. As I climbed higher and higher up an open ski run, the clouds had golden hems. The trees, too, I thought, had just such colors. I reached the top of the run and went on deep into the woods along the trail we had taken. I couldn't see the bright clouds anymore. The day seemed darker, as if half an hour had passed in a second. But the sky straight above me—what I could see of it through the leaves—was still light blue. I walked on and on, ever looking to the right, for I remembered that the cabin was on that side. The trail seemed narrower now than in the winter and it wasn't as easy to follow as when there'd been tracks in the snow. Tall maples and birches stood on each side of it and rustled in the wind. It's like music, I thought, the music I like best.

Despite the knapsack, I felt light and free, felt almost like skipping along. The trail followed the ridge, up and down and curving. Downhill at times I broke into a run; uphill I took the short, slow steps of mountaineers. Sometimes I paused and listened. I heard only the wind and once or twice a branch scraping on another—a sound that also was the wind's. The birds had gone to sleep. Soon I'll be asleep too, I thought—if I can find the cabin. I'd had supper in the village, and having got up very early that day,

I expected I wouldn't have any trouble sleeping. Maybe I'd light a fire, sip some of the apricot brandy I carried in my knapsack, and then go to bed.

After a few miles, before it was quite dark, I came to the cabin. It was just where I had thought it was—about 50 feet off the trail on the right—and I congratulated myself on my memory and sense of direction. Like the trail, it looked less prominent than in winter. It was almost hidden by the leaves, its wood weathered gray and brown and rather shaggy. The door was wide open and I went in. I shone my flashlight around. Though bare and primitive, the place was quite clean. There was the bunk, there the shelf, and there the fireplace with ashes and cinders, perhaps the same left by the fire that my friends and I had lit.

I set the knapsack on the floor, unrolled the blanket and laid it on the bunk, then went out to gather firewood. Soon I had a good bundle of twigs and deadwood and a strip of birch bark. They were dry and caught easily, the birch bark burning even better than paper. The chimney drew well, just as I remembered. I closed the door with some difficulty—the latch was loose. Then I sat gazing at the flames, reached for the apricot brandy, and took a few swigs of it. The flames leaped and danced. My shadow danced to them on the walls. The wood crackled, I stayed up till it had burned itself out. "And now I'll go to bed," I whispered. It was strange to hear my own voice. I took my shoes off. The bunk was hard. There was no mattress, but wrapped in my blanket—a soft blue English plaid—I felt snug. I closed my eyes, and, turning around, I settled on my right side as I usually do before going to sleep. I opened my eyes again to see if any of the embers still glowed in the fireplace. None did. The place was absolutely dark, and I closed my eyes again. The wind had died down. It was so quiet and still in the cabin I could hear the sound of my heart and my breathing.

But something seemed odd. I heard a sound of breathing—not in time with my own, but slower, and deeper. I stopped breathing—I don't know whether from anxiety or to make sure I wasn't mistaken. The sound went on. I wanted to jump out of the bunk, but I lay perfectly still, barely breathing, as if the slightest motion might give me away. The breathing was coming from below the bunk, and it was peaceful, regular, and deep—the breathing of someone sleeping soundly. That, at least, was reassuring, and I took a big breath. But still I didn't move. I couldn't seem to.

Who was it? What was it? Was it an animal? It must be an animal. No human would sleep *under* the bunk. Was it a raccoon? A skunk? No, it must be something larger. I couldn't remember hearing a cat—a healthy cat—breathe. They made practically no sound. A bear? Could it possibly be a bear? Yes, very possibly, I told myself, and thought of the open door and the loose latch. And yet it might be something smaller, and I wasn't going to leave my warm bunk, my cozy cabin, for a raccoon. I wasn't going to be made a fool of by some small creature, I had to find out. Where was my flashlight? Where were my shoes? Slowly I uncovered myself. And very carefully my fingers inched along the floor searching for the flashlight. I couldn't find it. I made wider and wider arcs with my fingers and at last reached it. I brought it up onto the bunk and lit it. Perhaps I shouldn't shine it under the bunk. No, definitely I should not. Again I put my hand on the floor and moved it even more gently than before toward the hollow under the bunk. But I found it impossible to move my fingers inward more than a couple of inches, and not because there was anything in my way. It was the unknown.

I clutched the flashlight and, muffling it with my hand, I brought it over the edge of the bunk and hung my head down. The breathing went on unruffled, and I took courage. But still I was too high. Was the animal hibernating? But wasn't it too early in the season for animals to hibernate? Whatever it was doing, it must have had a very large meal for it to sleep so soundly. Leaning out and down farther and farther and shining the flashlight under the bunk,

I saw fur—black, mountainous—obviously a bear's. Instantly I recoiled and in doing this struck the flashlight sharply against the edge of the bunk. There was a terrific knock under me. The whole bunk seemed to heave. It quaked, throwing me off balance against the wall. And the animal got out from under the bunk and stood on its paws in the middle of the floor between me and the door, a black bear so big I wondered how it could have fit under there. It shook sleep off like a dog shakes off water. Recovering somewhat, I shone the light in his eyes and he blinked as if dazed. I tried to be brave, I got out of the bunk and stood my ground. Any sign of fear on my part, I thought, and he would bound forth and claw me apart like a plaything. Where were my shoes? I didn't know where my shoes were. But there was my knapsack. I grabbed it by its metal frame and held it in front of me like a shield. He nudged it with his muzzle, perhaps smelling the food inside it, and held it with his forepaws.

"Good, bear, be good," I said in a soft, warm, imploring voice.

He rubbed his nose against the side of the knapsack harder and harder and tugged at it with his paws.

I was born and had grown up in Italy till I was 14, and somehow it came more natural for me in a crisis to speak in Italian. "*Buono,*" I said, "*stai buono.*" But the Italian didn't help, and in a mixture of Italian and English I went on, "*buono* now, good, good boy, *buono,* be quiet, gently now, good, good bear."

I had in my knapsack a large chocolate bar, a slice of cake, a loaf of bread, and a package of cheese. I pulled the loaf out, unwrapped it in a hurry, and gave it to him. He gorged it down as if I'd given him a crumb. I gave him the cheese. I gave him the chocolate bar. I gave him the cake. Soon everything was gone. Only the apricot brandy remained, and it was on the floor by the fireplace. I reached for it, and there, incidentally, were my shoes. I slipped into them, opened the bottle, and poured the syrupy fluid all out onto the hearth. He lapped it up with some relish. And now he looked at me. I had nothing else to give him.

He came closer. "*Buono, buono,*" I said, moving toward the door. I opened it. "Go home now, go." But he didn't move. And suddenly I thought: He *is* home; this isn't my house; this is his. And while he stood contentedly watching me, I picked up my blanket and holding onto my knapsack, empty now except for my toothbrush and a change of clothes, I returned to the doorway. He didn't follow me. He looked at me sadly, as at a departing guest, and turned toward the bunk. Slowly he crept under it. And I thought: He's going back to sleep, drugged by the brandy; I could get back to the bunk, too, but no—I would never sleep.

I made my way back to the trail, and along the trail to the ski run, and down the ski run to the village and the lodge. I got a room there. In the lounge people were drinking and dancing. I wandered among them. I sat at the bar hoping to find someone to tell my story to, but no one seemed right. When the bartender asked me what I would have, I ordered a glass of apricot brandy. I drank it and then went to bed between fresh sheets, with a telephone on the bedside table and a private bath opposite. I switched the light out. And still I couldn't sleep. I went to the window and looked at the mountain; for a long time I watched it. The moon, a gibbous moon, was lighting it now, and the moon mist hung over the village. I thought of the thousands of creatures in some kind of shelter or home for the night. "Home, home, everyone where he belongs," I said to myself, "lair, nest, cradle, bunk, bed."

"Bed," I repeated, getting back into it and closing my eyes.

the cove

Oscar was, by several weeks, the first of four students to arrive at Laniel, a village on Lake Kippawa in Quebec near the Ontario border, some 300 miles northwest of Montreal, where he went to college. He was going to work at a forestry department lab near the village. His was a summer job that his biology teacher had gotten him.

He had taken an express train west out of Montreal, and at Mattawa changed to a local that headed north along the Ottawa River toward James Bay. He felt adventurous, full of expectation, and fairly pleased with himself to have found what seemed to him an important, well-paying job. But as the conductor of the local came to check his ticket, he realized that he was missing his wallet with the ticket in it; and self-reproach, misgivings, and worry took the place of his gladness. The conductor, a lean, white-haired man, was very understanding. He said his wallet must have slipped out of his pocket on the express train. There was nothing to worry about. At the next station—in a few minutes—he would talk to the stationmaster. The stationmaster would telephone North Bay, where the express was due shortly, and he'd get his wallet in the morning on the next train up. Such things happened all the time. He'd let him know as soon as they got to Temiskaming. Oscar smiled more in gratitude than hope—in matters of this sort he was rather pessimistic—and resumed looking at the steep, wooded banks of the Ottawa River. A while ago their beauty had stirred him, but now he drew no comfort from them. At Temiskaming the conductor, his face emotionless, came to tell him that the wallet was found. "You'll have it back tomorrow morning," he added.

"That's wonderful! Thank you," Oscar said and, hardly able to contain his joy, rose and shook the man's hand; he praised the railroad and Canada, and might have gone on to include mankind, the world, and heaven, too, had not the conductor, turning from so much praise, gone on down the aisle.

Now the river glistened again, the leaves shone, and—when he reached Laniel—far from being ashamed of himself, he had a joyful story to tell the head of the lab who had come to meet him at the station.

The head of the lab, Larry, was a soft-spoken, lanky young man. Wearing a tartan shirt with rolled-up sleeves, he greeted Oscar with a strong handshake and a genuine, disarming, absolutely unartificial smile. He seemed to have a slight stoop to his shoulders, perhaps because of his height or from long hours over a microscope—he was an expert on budworms, the insects which in their various stages, from egg to larva to moth, infest large portions of the Canadian woods, especially balsam. He turned to a very pretty brunette and introduced them. She was his wife, Jessica. Side by side, his arm around her, they reminded Oscar of pictures he had seen of man and wife in ancient Egyptian art—the same cheerful expression of two who look to the future serenely.

The village was small—just a few rows of houses, warehouses, a garage that belonged to the lab, two or three stores, a lumber mill, and a dock on the lake near the station. They boarded a motorboat. The engine started after one smart pull of the flywheel, and with a whining noise that tore up the silence, they were off and speeding along the broadening bay, the bow furiously cleaving the still, limpid water, to a point on the rocky shore about a quarter of a mile distant. They landed at a wharf where another boat and two canoes were tied up. A slight, spare, sinewy middle-aged man greeted them. His name was Théophile and he was from Laniel. "Théophile keeps the place going—the cars, the boats. . . . He built everything here, and he's a very good cook," Larry said.

"The pickup need a new gasket," Théophile said in a Quebecois accent. Then, turning to Oscar, "You didn't have no supper."

"How can you tell?" Larry asked.

"He look hungry. And no food in the train either, that I know."

"Even if there were, he wouldn't have been able to buy it. Left his wallet on the express. But it was found—it'll be here with the early train. Could you pick it up at the stationmaster's when you come in tomorrow morning?"

"His wallet? Sure," Théophile said, taking a critical look at him.

"Thank you," Oscar said.

They showed him to a cabin with a bunk, and then to the kitchen, which also served as dining room and sitting room, in a building that faced the lake. Théophile heated some ham and beans in a pan, then laid it on the table, all the time talking to Larry about things that had to be done. "Well, I go now," he said, wished them good night, and left for the village in one of the boats.

Larry and Jessica answered Oscar's questions about the lake. It was large and had many islands and bays. Its coastline was so irregular, it measured more than a thousand miles. It stretched east for seventy miles and branched north and south a long way. The lab was at its westernmost corner. Larry and Jessica lived nearby—a ten-minute walk from the lab—on the next point of land on the lake in a log cabin Larry had built. For five or six weeks, they told him, he'd be alone here at night, then three more students were going to come—high school students, who didn't finish school till the middle of June. "You won't mind being alone?" Larry asked.

"Oh no, I won't mind."

"If you need anything, just come over to our place. Along that path. You can't miss it," Larry said, and they left.

Only then did he fully appreciate the silence around him. It seemed like a voice from which all sounds are born. He listened to it and watched the night gradually intensify and assert itself. Never before had he had such a large place all to himself. He stepped outside and smelled the night. It had its own perfume. Sunlight expressed a different fragrance. This was subtler, sweeter. It partook of the night's velvety texture. He descended to the level of the lake and touched the water, then dipped his arms deep into it. The surface around them was like imagined bracelets. He returned to the kitchen and sat by the lamp for a time, then he went to his cabin.

He slept soundly and rose at dawn, in time to watch the morning quicken, the light gradually reassert itself over darkness, the night recede. He walked down to the lake, which was shrouded in mist. As though it were breathing, vapor rose from it, making it look more alive. Then, as the sun rose, the mist slowly lifted or vanished, and the other side of the bay was disclosed, narrowing toward Laniel at his right, but widening to his left, point after point, its cliffs fringed with pines. Above him a bird flew diagonally across the lake, uttering a strange, hollow, prolonged, and melodious cry, the like of which he had never heard but was to hear again and again through the summer. It was a loon. Its song had something human and nonhuman about it. The water was at this time of the year—late spring—too cold to swim in at leisure, but he dove in nevertheless, then quickly returned to the wharf and his cabin. He made coffee in the kitchen; it was the first time he had ever kept house.

At eight, Théophile came with Oscar's wallet for him, and then Larry arrived. They all went out into the woods with clippers and baskets to gather balsam branches, which they took to the lab where Larry showed him how to spot diseased balsam needles. He and Larry counted them and entered the numbers in a notebook. In the days that followed, they roved the forest, on foot, or in a pickup truck or by boat, clipping the samples. Later, as the larvae grew, they examined them under a microscope for possible parasites with the hope of finding a viable, prolific, and virulent one that could be cultured and then spread over the forest. The work was tedious, but their expeditions were not, especially those on the lake. They went to remote bays and sometimes camped out for one or more nights. He sensed the vastness of the land, that to the north stretched boundless toward a distant sea and the islands of the Arctic. Once, a moose drinking at an inlet, its massive head crowned with antlers, looked at them then galloped away

the cove

47

dripping water. Another time, while they were driving down
a road in the woods, a bear crossed fast in front of them;
and that appearance, though momentary, was more instruc-
tive than minutes spent watching bears in zoos or hours
spent reading about them in zoology textbooks. And always,
after these expeditions, it was good to return to the lab, the
kitchen, his cabin, his bunk. Within walking distance of
the lab, he found a little lake. It was in a hollow that re-
flected the green of the forest around it more than the blue
of the sky. The water was clear and it rippled and shone.
Again and again, after work in the evening, he went to this
lake. It seemed virgin and secret. If there was no wind,
each leaf was faithfully portrayed, but the lightest breeze
would cancel each image. He would watch the wayward,
playful wind ruffling the surface, drawing arabesques, losing itself, finding itself again. And in the big lake he would
go out by himself with the powerful outboard, at high speed,
in the deep water under the sheer cliffs, weaving his way
between rocks. Once, he struck one that lay under the surface and the motor went dead. He thought he had smashed
the propeller. Feeling contrite, he rowed back to shore.
"You probably just broke the point," Théophile said, and in
a jiffy replaced it. Even more than going on the outboard,
he liked canoeing. One of the canoes was made of birch
bark; the other, of aluminum, could be fitted with a sail.
With them he could steal into the shallowest water and
silently explore caves and recesses. Often he went into the
village, either by boat or—though it was much longer—on
foot by a path that skirted the lake. But there wasn't much
to do there. The villagers kept to themselves; and he didn't
find it easy to talk to them, although he spoke some
French. There, when he heard a train, he would go to the
station for the link to the rest of the world it provided and
watch the passengers though they sat behind glass and
hardly any of them ever got off at Laniel. One morning he
got up to find the end of the lake, all the way to the village,
solid with logs. They had been chained together and drawn

by a tugboat to the dock, where they would be loaded onto a freight train. For days the logs floated there, leaving only a narrow channel for boats. He learned to logroll. From log to log he crossed the lake. And he learned to chop wood, splitting a log with one ax blow.

It was fun, but he would have had more fun with a friend. His need to see new faces, unappeased by his trips to the village, grew intense. A drive to Temiskaming for supplies was a rare, exciting treat, though Temiskaming was only a small town. In midsummer, Larry said, they would drive south to North Bay and perhaps north to Cobalt and Cochrane. The mere mention of these towns filled Oscar with wonder. At one point Larry announced that a government official from the forestry department was going to come for a short visit, and the expectation that the news stirred was as pitiful as it was fantastic. But when the man finally arrived the joy of seeing him was inexplicably brief. The man wasn't particularly dull; nonetheless, after an hour or two, Oscar wanted to see someone else. One person made him all the more aware of the others he was missing, and served more to kindle than quench his desire for new faces. In a week or so, Fred, a geneticist (his idea, according to Larry, was to breed a budworm that was sexually attractive to the others, yet barren) with his wife, Theresa, was going to join the staff and live in a shack beyond Larry's and Jessica's log cabin. Again the sense of expectation, heightened by the thought of a new woman around. They came, and the woman was beautiful. For a while his solitude vanished; then as he watched them disappear down the path on their way to the shack, it returned. They were so smug, the two couples, there in the shack and log cabin; and they made such a show of their togetherness that they, too, rather than provide company, increased his awareness of being alone.

Then it was mid-June and the three high school students arrived—Steve and Bill from Ottawa on one train,

the cove

49

and Mark from Kingston on a later train. Bill and Steve, from the same school and long-time friends, were both rather vapid, but casual and natural; they took an immediate disliking to Mark who, though about the same age, had the staid look of an adult. They thought he was stodgy, prissy—a know-it-all. He did have a way of making you feel that whatever you said to him was hardly worth saying. Oscar tried to bring the three together but failed. Nor did things improve with time. Hearing their foolish quarrels and insults, he wished he were alone again. And yet it was good to have someone to talk to, and good to canoe and swim with them. Despite his reproaching them for the way they treated Mark, Steve and Bill liked him. Oscar felt that they regarded him as something of a character, an interesting oddity, with his walks to the little lake, the poetry books he kept on his bedside table, his musings, his rapt wonder at nature. And he was a little older and stronger than they. He could swim faster and farther and dared go into the lake no matter how hard the wind blew. There was something slightly reckless about him, which they admired. And he had ideas that never occurred to them: washing clothes by stringing them in a long line that he pulled around the lake with the outboard, inviting them all to a little dinner party on top of a disused fire tower, sawing a pair of water skis out of a tree trunk, making a weather vane with a shingle, paddling and portaging to the Ottawa River, riding a freight train to the next station down. Though he didn't feel very amusing, the three of them depended on him for company. But when he suggested going into the village in the hope of meeting some girls, Bill and Steve reacted with a nervous snicker, Mark with a disparaging and only momentary look away from a detective story. The local girls seemed to scare them even more than high winds.

Was it that the girls in Laniel appeared to be very reserved and not at all inclined to talk to outsiders like them? Was it snobbishness? Was it that they didn't speak French? Or was it that girls, women, were still beyond them? There was something strangely neutral about them. When he spoke in glowing terms about Jessica and Theresa, they hardly replied. They just didn't seem to speculate about love—or they had taken a break from it here. And yet they were seventeen and eighteen. They might have had girl friends back home, but if so they never talked about them and hardly ever wrote or received any letters.

Oscar, on the other hand, longed for love to liven his life. He thought of a girl in his Greek class at college, of two girls he had skied with in the Laurentians, of one he had met while picking fruit the summer before in the Niagara peninsula. Though he had taken these and others out he had never had an affair and felt ashamed of his innocence. It was a state he wanted to molt from. The boys would call him to join them down at the lake or to play a game of horseshoes, and, though painfully aware that such pleasures were trifles compared to love, he went along.

Sometimes, however, tired of their company, he walked into the village alone, hoping for a happy encounter. It was the middle of August now, but since Laniel was not a summer resort, it looked no different; there was no more movement than before. One day, though, on the path that skirted the lake, halfway between the lab and the village, behind a wooden gate in the backyard of a cottage, he saw a girl, quite tall, with a large face and tawny hair. She wasn't doing anything in particular, just standing there outside the open door of the cottage. As he approached to go past the gate, she looked at him with the same curiosity, he thought, with which he was looking at her. Perhaps in this lonely district new faces held as much interest for her as for him. He said hello and she smiled at him in the kindly, slightly condescending way that girls have with boys who are clearly younger than they. She must have been in her early twenties, a few years older than he. She wasn't exactly pretty—more handsome than pretty, and rather unusual. Her long tawny hair, her sandy complexion had something fairylike and bewitching. He paused.

"Are you from the lab?" she asked.

"Yes, and you are vacationing here?"

"Yes, and to look after my father. He's not well."

"Oh, I'm sorry. I hope it's not serious."

"No, he had a fall, at the mill."

Through the open door and a window across from it he could see the lake, and frilly curtains and polished furniture—so different from the roughhewn, heavy tables and chairs at the lab. Flowers grew in the small, narrow backyard. Morning glories seemed to float in the air next to the wall. "This is a nice house," he said. "Right on the edge of the lake, and so cozy compared to the lab."

"Yes, it's nice. But Laniel . . ."

"Are you from a big city?"

"No, not a big city. Sudbury."

"Still, there must be a lot going on there."

"No, not a lot, but a lot more than here."

"If you like, some evening I could take you out on the lab's outboard."

"A ride on the boat? Yes, I'd like that."

"When would you like to go? Tomorrow? Any day."

"Tomorrow'd be fine, if it's as hot as today."

"I could come here in front of your house after work, around six. And I'll get some food and wine in the village and we could have a picnic."

"Good," she said, and as he was about to go, she added, "Hey, I don't know your name."

"I'm Oscar, and I work at the lab. Oh, I've already said that! I go to college in Montreal."

"I'm Peggy, and I live with my mother and work in an office in Sudbury, Ontario." The amused, slightly condescending smile again lit her face, "I'll see you tomorrow," she said.

While she was still in sight he had to control his step, but when he had rounded a bend his step quickened to keep pace with his heart, with his life. Soon his walk broke into a lilt and a run. He raced to the lab. He slowed down as he climbed the steps to the kitchen. Bright-eyed and with a lingering smile he went in.

"What happened to you?" Steve said.

"Oh, nothing. Just *joie de vivre*. Such *joie de vivre* here in Laniel."

He kept his secret, he revelled in it, went to bed and woke up with it. In the lab he had a hard time counting the insects. He kept seeing her, through the microscope, as if it were a telescope that could peer around corners and behind walls. She was so confiding and friendly—and not a little mysterious behind her curtain of hair. After work he said he wasn't going to have dinner here.

"Where are you going?" Bill asked him.

"I'm going out with a girl."

They looked at him as if they couldn't believe him. Who was she? Where? How had he met her? Where was he going to take her? He just smiled. "Tell us," they said as he went down to the boat.

For an answer he tugged at the flywheel, and was gone. First, he went to Laniel for bread, cheese, olives, and wine. At six he pulled alongside the float in front of her house. He knocked at the door on the lake side. A man's voice asked him in. He opened the door and saw a man well past middle age in an arm chair, his leg in a cast and a pair of crutches beside him. "Peggy'll be ready in a minute. She's in the kitchen. I just finished supper. Sit down." After telling him that he was glad Peggy had found a friend, and cautioning about boats and especially outboards, he said a few words about his leg, then began talking about the work ethic. Oscar was not interested in working hours but in those certain moments that enclose eternity in them—and sometimes disclose it. He listened dutifully, nevertheless, until the door was opened with a flourish and Peggy appeared in a blouse and skirt.

"What was dad talking about?" she asked him on the way down to the boat.

the cove

53

"Work."

"Oh," she said and made a movement as though shrugging off a yoke. Then, taking his hand, she stepped into the boat.

They sped away. He wasn't sure where he would take her. First, they swept by the pier in Laniel, the wake making the boats in the harbor bob; then he skirted the coastline opposite the lab. The cliffs got higher. The bay widened. Two rocky headlands, weathered smooth by the ages, marked the entrance to a cove. He had been here before by boat and canoe. He cut the motor and they moved silently between the two narrowing cliffs whose shadows darkened the still and deep water. Ferns and pines grew on ledges up the cliffs' sides. Behind them, the open lake, still light and sunny, seemed like a window. Peggy looked up at the sky. There wasn't much of it. She was able to touch a fern that leaned out of the cliff wall. Then the keel brushed the sandy bottom, and they were still.

They stepped into the warm, clear water and he pulled the boat in. She was full of wonder at the beauty of the place. They both seemed to feel that no words could describe it, and so they just sat for a while—silent in the silence. He took the wine and food out of the boat and set it on the grass. When they spoke their voices sounded resonant, perhaps because the cove was shaped like a megaphone or a funnel. She sang a high note, and, pure as it was, it echoed even more pure. She sat with her hands clasped around her flexed knees, her skirt as taut as a tent and her feet barely touching the ground, in a posture that fascinated him; she looked like something he wanted to unravel. With her head slightly cocked she gazed at the water's surface as if she wanted to be level with it. "This sure beats staying home," she said.

He laughed joyfully at the indirect compliment. "What do you talk about with your dad?" he asked her.

"He's strong on work, as you know, and religion. He thinks if you apply yourself, you can get anywhere. He's such an optimist it's dismaying. I don't know why optimism should depress me, but it does. 'Everything's possible,' he keeps saying. 'Anything's within reach. Knock and it shall be opened unto you.' But I know it isn't so."

"I think one needs, each time, a very cleverly made, subtle, and fortunate key."

"Right," she said and grabbed his arm with enthusiasm. From his arm she brought her hand to her forehead to ward off a mosquito.

"Wait," he said. "In the boat there's something to keep them away." He went to the boat and brought back a little bottle. "Kippawa dope—keep-away dope—Larry's special preparation. He runs the lab and knows more about insects than anyone I've ever met. He's an authority, in fact. Let me rub some on you."

"How provident of you."

He daubed some of the ointment on her face, arms, and ankles. "Your legs, too," he said, and he gently rubbed the stuff on her shins and calves, up to her knees. She drew her skirt up over her knees. Carefully, as if he were touching something very precious, he rounded her knees. How smooth they felt! Lovingly, he spread the ointment as far up her thighs as he dared; still and passive, she let him. He felt like a doctor or a make-up man. Then he smeared some on himself.

"It works," she said.

"A magic balm."

He drew himself close to her. Slowly, very gradually, his mouth sought her mouth. He noted the pungent smell of balsam and soon forgot it. He pressed her lips. Yielding to the kiss, she reclined on the grass. Closer and closer they lay. And later, much later, they swam in their nakedness.

"I love love," she said.

It was dark now. The night hid them. A firefly glowed, an ephemeral star. It left a wake of light, then became invisible. Again, it shone in the distance. "Their light hasn't been fully explained," he told her.

"I'm glad," she said.

They reclined again. The darkness made touch more important. With that one sense he perceived her. "I wonder how many other creatures are making love in these woods."

"Thousands," she said.

"They are our brothers and sisters."

An envious wind stirred the branches. High above them, on the top of the cliff, they heard the pines soughing.

When he returned to the lab the boys were playing cards—Mark, too, who had never played with them before. Though he felt they had waited up for him, they didn't stop playing. They barely looked at him: not like a stranger, he felt, for they would have looked at a stranger, but rather like someone whom they knew and who had changed, had suddenly grown a bit older, all of a sudden a bit, and left them behind. The distance between them was more than the three or four feet that separated them. It was as if he were standing on the other side of a rift.

The rift widened each time he saw her. The lake, the woods—which had been so much in the foreground—became background scenery, and she stood, or lay, prominent and always new, either at her home or on the grass of the cove, or on the smooth rocks lapped by the tideless water, or on a tiny island where only a few stunted pines grew in crevices, or on the boat. At times, especially at night, alone on his bunk thinking of her, she seemed immense, dwarfing everything else. Her town—Sudbury—became a huge center for him. Could he go there? Could she come to Montreal? Endlessly, he debated the questions, till they put him to sleep.

One evening he took her to the lab. Steve and Bill giggled and Mark flushed, as they met her.

"They've got such limp handshakes," she said later. "Sweaty, too—Mark's."

"Hmm. But Mark, whom I never thought of as handsome, as he looked at you and blushed, seemed so. He looked positively splendid; his pimples were as red as miniature volcanoes erupting."

"Really? I can only remember those clammy hands."

"They were scared."

"What were they scared of?"

"Beauty."

He was all faith and service and in his free time did whatever she wanted. If she wanted him to play chess, he played chess. If she wished he would talk to her father, he talked to him. If she wanted to go out, he took her out. He felt like the weather vane he had made.

"You are so agreeable," she remarked.

"I am easily swayed."

"Too easily," she said and gave him a little push. He feigned a fall, and an amused, slightly derisive smile lit her face.

Closer and closer to her, farther and farther away from the boys, he drifted, till the summer was about over and the time came to leave.

"I've been wondering," she said; "perhaps we should think of this as just one long boat ride—a shipboard romance."

"No, the outboard isn't a ship and the lake isn't an ocean."

"But in a way it's the same. There was a boat and a time limit, as in an ocean crossing. And now the cruise has come to an end. You have to go back to your life. I have to go back to mine."

How was it that one discordant note could turn to nothing what had seemed founded on rock, what had looked as though it could never be shattered? He couldn't say a word. He got a shrinking, tightening feeling and a mad, useless urge to hang on.

"Will you write to me?" she said, assuming the air of the older person he had noticed in her at the beginning.

"Yes," he said, and he remembered his correspondences and how they would flourish for only a short season, to dwindle and fade like wild flowers. "'The sweetest flowers are ever frail and rare,'" he said, "'And love and freedom blossom but to wither.'" There he was, screening himself behind quotations. He kissed her, and there was a bitter taste in his mouth—a taste of tears, a dryness.

From Montreal he wrote to her. It was a long time before he got a reply, and it was preceded by a letter from Steve—a tedious letter about what he and Bill were doing. Her letter was similar, was no reply at all, and in vain he looked for more warmth in it than the words "dear" at the beginning and "love" at the end carried in them.

"She was obviously much more important to you than you were to her," a friend at college told him. The words had the unwelcome ring of unacceptable truth.

He looks at Lake Kippawa on the map. It is a jagged blue spot so small he has trouble finding it again if his eyes stray from it a moment. And then he looks for Sudbury. It is a name in little letters beside a tiny dot. "Once," he tells himself, "the rest of the world looked small, not these places."

the foghorn

I was sailing from Canada to England after the
war, one of ten passengers aboard a freighter. In
the cabin next to mine there was a child with her
mother. They were on their way home from Singa-
pore, where the Japanese had interned them. The
child was a little girl of four, frail and gentle as only
little girls can be. I was with them in the lounge
when we entered the fog banks of Newfoundland
and the ship's horn began blowing. Loud, long,
and dismal bellows it made. The first one seemed
especially long. It couldn't have lasted more than a

few seconds, yet it seemed it would never cease. Loud and disturbing, they came at regular intervals, making the minutes of silence in between seem short and irrelevant.

The horn reminded the little girl of the sirens that announced air raids, or perhaps the roll calls in the camp. Every time it blew, she screamed and frantically hugged her mother for shelter.

Now, it takes a long time for a ship to cross the fog banks of Newfoundland.

Hard as her mother tried to explain to her that there was no danger of air raids or roll calls, the child couldn't help crying each time the horn blew. Her little windpipe accompanied the huge, monstrous one of the ship, and the low note and the high note mingled to make a strident duet.

How long would it last? I went on deck and looked down for the sea, but I couldn't see it. I looked up for the sky. There was no sky, only gray denseness. I looked in front of me for clear spaces, but there were none—only fog and no break in the fog; different thicknesses of it sometimes, that was all; cloudlets within a cloud, clouds within an overcast sky, all moving at sea level, cleft only by the shape of a ship and the sound of a horn drowning the screams of a child.

Would it never cease? I felt like going up to ask the captain if he wouldn't please stop it. After all, he had radar now, hadn't he? Of course he had; there it was, the vane, turning, revolving, peering through miles of fog. I could see it—or, rather, I could make it out. But I also knew that in this weather it was regulation to blow the foghorn.

There seemed no remedy. The little girl didn't get used to the horn. It seemed she never would. It seemed she would go on and on till she screamed herself to exhaustion. The silent minutes seemed to come not to quiet her or bring her relief but to let her recover her voice for the next sound.

It seemed cruel—it seemed cruel that now peace had come, there shouldn't be peace for her. For her the war had not ended. It was still going on. Echoes of it, out of time, out of place, like a swarm of wasps, still pursued her.

Her mother was carrying her out of the lounge, ineffectually trying to console her, when I stopped them and asked the child's mother if she would let me try. She gave the little girl to me, and I held her in my right arm. I got on my knees and put my left hand on the floor. With my right I placed her on my back. She put her arms around my neck, and I went down on all fours.

"I am a pony now and you are a lady on horseback," I said.

I remember one of the passengers' telling me I would get my trousers dirty. I neighed angrily at him.

She was a good rider, I found. Her knees hugged my ribs tightly.

"That's right, hug on tight," I said.

"You aren't supposed to talk; you are a pony," she replied.

I went round the lounge once; then I stopped. She spurred my chest with her heels, and pulled my hair with her nervous little hands.

"Go on," she said.

"Not till I hear the signal," I replied.

"What signal?"

"The horn blowing, that's my signal."

She sat still and silent. I could sense that she was deep in thought.

"The horn?" she said, perplexedly. "Is that your signal?"

"Yes."

It was due to blow now at any moment. I waited, she waited, her mother waited. We all looked at each other, waiting. Rarely, I think, have I gone through such suspense. Then it blew, and I trotted forth, and she wasn't crying.

At the end of the sound, I stopped. When the horn was about to blow again, I got set and repeated the sequence. This we did three or four times. At each signal I sprang forth like a race horse when the starting gate is lifted. She loved it. If I felt that she was about to fall, I would bring an arm up and steady her. At the next interval—the fourth or the fifth, whichever it was—I got up and we held hands. I told her the pony was tired. The suspense—for me, at least—was even greater this time.

But when the horn blew at last, she was smiling. Later, if I remember correctly, we had another run. She was laughing. By showing her how to put a finger in front of her mouth and blow on it, buzzing and humming against it, I even got her to imitate the sound of the horn.

the park

The park was laid out about 1840 on a slope facing
north at the end of a long cypress drive from the
Tuscan villa. The villa itself is also of that time—
a large, three-floor white intonaco house. A bit dull
from the outside: four plain walls with three rows
of windows. Too many windows, perhaps. It has a
front yard enclosed by a tall wall, on top of which
is a spiky, hostile, silvery railing. You enter the yard
through an immense gate, very pretentious, painted
silver like the railing and topped with a similar pat-
tern of lancelike spikes. The roadway to the front

door is surfaced with tiny white pebbles. On each side stand cedars, firs, palms, and persimmons, the last tantalizingly close to the wall.

You feel wealth all around you, and also a sense of something too private and formal—a sense that increases if you ring the bell. Then a waiter in white gloves and striped jacket comes to open the door. He leads you over polished tile floors to a carpeted salon, rather gloomy despite the elegant furniture, vases, and other good things of the period. Not enough sunlight; the silver, the shiny chandeliers not enough to make up for its lack. On the other side of the house is the garden, with a fountain in the center and a symmetrical design of flower beds, an attractive orangery to one side, roses climbing the walls, and in huge pots tall lemon trees laden with fruit. Then there is the long cypress drive, and—what the villa is best known for—the park at the end of the drive.

A gentle, deeply religious, titled old couple had inherited the estate. They died childless about 1950, leaving it to a young niece who, even when she later got married and had a little boy, preferred living in town and spent only a few weeks in the summer at the villa. People said that the first thing her husband wanted to do after taking stock of the place was cut down the cypresses to sell as timber. With difficulty, wife, friends, bailiff, and farmers persuaded him not to. Over the years, with the shortage and increasingly high cost of labor, the park was left more or less to itself. It certainly wasn't kept up the way it used to be when the old couple was living. Then there were waterworks all in perfect condition, such as a fountain with tall jets of water and stepping stones, and a well that sprinkled you the moment you looked into it and the host stepped on a lever. At the "hermitage"—really the house of the gardener—a wooden hermit friar on wheels rolled toward you when you opened the door. There were a Chinese hut, an open-air theatre with mossy stone seats and a hedged stage, a wooden bridge, a long trellised gallery, statues with inscriptions, a grotto, a spring, a brook, a boxwood maze. And, down deep in the park, seven sequoias, imported from California and planted around 1840—the biggest trees in the neighborhood and perhaps in all Europe. The hermit is still there, but he doesn't roll anymore when you open the door. The Chinese hut has caved in. The bridge is unsteady. Some of the paths are overgrown. The park has the air of an abandoned garden, and perhaps it has improved with age. It has become more mysterious, and it may be just as well that the waterworks are not in perfect condition.

Though hardly anyone ever goes there, the park is open to visitors. No admission ticket is required, or anything like that. You just go to the gardener's cottage—the hermitage—by a little country road that skirts the cypress drive, and the gardener's wife, who is usually upstairs in the kitchen, will let you in. Once in a while, her ten-year-old daughter will offer to show you around. She's a sweet child, quite unobtrusive, and leads you as a kitten might. Sometimes you think you've lost her, but she appears a moment later ahead of you among the leaves. You are hardly aware of her presence. Back at the entrance, you leave her or her mother a tip.

One afternoon last August, two visitors went to the park. They were staying as paying guests at another villa nearby. He—a zealous student from England, with glasses and curly brown hair—was eighteen and looked twenty-three. She—blond, nimble, and pretty—thirty-eight and looked twenty. An American divorcée with large, thoughtful eyes, she seemed to gaze beyond you at her fifteen years of marriage to an economist she hardly loved, who drank and abused her and who very recently, soon after the divorce, had married a model, much younger. At times she seemed to regret having left him—she kept saying how extremely successful he was, despite his drunkenness. The other guests looked at her, graceful in her fresh summer dresses, of which she seemed to have an endless supply, and wondered how any man could be so foolish as to cause her to leave him. The boy knew some Italian, she hardly a word. She had been at the villa a week; he two months, taking a course at the academy of music in town. He was a flutist, and very intense and serious about it, practicing many hours every day, and sometimes playing for the guests after supper in the garden. When he practiced, the music filled a good part of the house, but he played so well that no one minded. "I love to hear him, especially when he practices. Then it sounds so natural—almost like hearing the birds," she said one evening, and, turning to him, she asked, "Do the birds sound very different to you?"

"Only the cuckoo's notes have any resemblance," he said.

Though his teacher in town was a world celebrity, the young man wasn't satisfied, and his parents, both of whom were well-known musicians in London, often called long distance and urged him to leave. But he liked the villa, had struck up quite a friendship with the American divorcée, and was staying on against his parents' advice.

"I'm told there's a park near here," he said to her. "I've never been there, but I know where it is and we could go over together if you like. They say it's the most unusual thing around."

"I'd love to see it," she replied in her very feminine voice. "But won't that take you away from your practicing?"

He shrugged. "It's probably good for me to have a break."

She smiled, obviously pleased that one his age should pay her so much attention and be willing to put his flute aside for a whole afternoon—something he had not done since they had met. So assiduous was he in his work, he told her, that he had never even been inside the famous cathedral in town or seen the museums. She gazed at him warmly—protectively, too. Her glances were lambent, not burning. She always seemed aware he was only eighteen.

It was an oppressively hot day, the sky glary, the atmosphere heavy, and this was another good reason for going to the park. She had a rented car, and in good American style they drove to the hermitage though it was no more than a mile away. They parked on the country road, opposite the gardener's cottage.

"Hello!" he called, and the gardener's wife—a pleasant young woman with a kerchief round her head—appeared at the top of an outside staircase on the second floor. She came down, led them through the hermit's bedroom, living room, and kitchen, showed them the venerable old wooden man, his loaf of bread, cheese, wine decanter, Bible, bunk bed, and pillow, all made of painted terra-cotta, and then let them into the park and left them on their own.

High above them were the thick fronds of an ilex. They couldn't see the sky, and the shade was unbroken except for a spot of sunlight that would show up, disappear, and return for a moment.

The family that first conceived of the park, and its direct descendants right on down to the deceased, childless old couple, had been very devout people, and the two visitors, who had already sensed the religious tone pervading the place from a Latin verse from the Scriptures at the entrance of the hermitage and from the presence of the hermit with his Bible, gained an even stronger impression of it as they went down a steep path that, every few yards, had a step and a cross with Roman numerals on it, representing the twelve Stations of the Cross. Beyond them, the path become mossy. An inviolate silence reigned, which the rare sound of a bird seemed only to consecrate. The sun hardly entered. The garish light outside here became a delicate green. It was refreshingly cool. They walked lightly over the live velvet softness along the path that led gently down the slope. Ferns brushed their arms. They came to a wall with the statue of an angel in a niche, and below it a weathered marble slab with an inscription. There was moss on it, and fungi, and part of it was blackened by the moisture oozing from the slope, but the carved words could still be made out, and he slowly read and translated:

Enter into these woods, whoever you are. Wander, if you like, along these shady paths. If you are tired, rest on the rough-hewn seats and the fresh grass. Visit the hermitage, the hut, the grotto, the font at your leisure. Walk freely wherever you will, but beware lest you commit any sin and thereby incur the wrath of the Lord. Even as the lily is at home here, let any impure act be alien.

They laughed at the "beware lest you commit any sin."

"That's rather nice. 'Even as the lily is at home here,'" he said. "But how do you like the 'any impure act'?"

"I don't," she said, and laughed faintly, while he laughed with the wistful relish of one who hasn't yet managed to shed as much of his innocence as he would like to.

Soon they came to another statue, this one of a child. A plaque said that this little monument was in her memory, and gave her name—the surname that of the founder's family—and the dates, pitifully close in time. In single file they walked under the rusty arcs of the trellis all covered with vine, then, holding hands, across the wooden bridge over a leaf-strewn gully, and down to the theatre, which not only was cushioned with moss but had little flowers and ferns growing out of cracks in the stone where earth had gathered. He went around the hedge and onto the stage. He looked at her—an audience so special that for a moment he felt stagestruck. He wished he had his flute. Why hadn't he brought it? This was the place, the time, the audience for music. He decided: he would whistle for her a movement of the concerto he had been working on at the villa. Subtler than the flute, the music rose and fell to rise again, thin as the nectar of snapdragons, and as sweet. Her eyes held him. She was with him, now high, now low, wherever the notes took them—the notes that bridged the gap of years, that made nothing of it, that made everything seem possible.

At the end of the movement, they walked over to a grotto dug into a cliff. Water oozed from every stone; no wonder the vegetation was luxuriant. A spring gushed from the base of the cliff face, forming a pool. From there the water flowed down a grassy brook to feed the fountain, which, however, was no longer watertight. Nearby was the well, artless now. They bent forward and saw their reflections.

"Did you make a wish?" he said.

"Yes, did you?"

"I wished you well," he said, and laughed. "What did you wish?"

She didn't say, but, looking intently at him with her large, pensive eyes, came near and kissed him.

He leaned on the balustrade of the well to steady himself, silent because the new mood felt gossamer-frail, in danger of being torn by any word, any move. Taking him by the hand, in silence she walked with him to the sequoias. Like pillars of a gigantic temple, the trunks rose, furrowed, bare of branches, to the sky, and there, a good hundred feet up, their foliage spread—huge green limbs hovering over the forest. Their pinnacles grew in diamond-shaped crowns.

Slowly, almost languorously, they began walking back up the slope by a different route from the one they had taken on their way down. The path had not been cleared in a long time. Dead branches had fallen across it and lay rotting. The boxwood hedge, which had once been a cleverly designed maze, here needed clipping, there had wide gaps. All too easily they found their way out. A certain heaviness came over him that he couldn't account for. It was as if he were carrying up the incline a weight that rested not on his shoulders but on every cell of his body. Was it the weight of love? Was it the weight of years? Eighteen years—hardly a

the park

load. She, on the other hand, seemed to be walking more lightly, emerging from the depth of the forest ahead of him, airy. Once in a while, blithely, she turned to look at him. He felt a drop of rain and heard the distant rumble of thunder. They passed by the inscription again, and his eyes paused on the word "sin." Step by step they climbed up the Stations of the Cross to the level of the hermitage, and passed the quarters of the wooden, stodgy hermit to the other side, left a tip for the gardener's wife at the bottom of the staircase, and closed the gate behind them.

Out in the glary light and sultry atmosphere that the distant storm had done nothing to clear, he longed for the darkness of the wood. She, too, as she stepped into the car and took the wheel and shifted from neutral into first gear, became suddenly a practical creature coping with the mechanical world, cramped by it into an inelegant posture in which one machine-directed movement followed another without rhythm or grace. It was so unlike the way it had been in the park, where he had whistled like a faun and she had kissed him like a woodland fairy.

Back in the villa, strangely, she spoke of her children, whom she had hardly ever mentioned to him. They were going to be out of summer camp in a week, she said. She spoke of New York. She said that perhaps someday he would give a concert in New York and that she would go and see him. And less than an hour ago he had been under the illusion that they would never part. He looked at her blankly. Her eyes, her face, her lips. Again he heard the sound of thunder, a rumble in the distance, like a grumble, and he thought of the inscription again, and the word "sin." He wished that they *had* sinned and that the Lord had struck them dead with lightning at that instant. But they hadn't sinned. Not, surely, with a kiss? O God, he felt that with that kiss she had placed on his mouth a seal or an enchantment to prevent that he should ever draw from other lips pleasure or sweetness or content, or slake his thirst for love.

to mock the years

I have a tendency to fall in love with women older than I am, sometimes much older, as long as beauty keeps them young and will not fade. I love the mockery they make of time, the way they flout the years or check their advance. It seems to me that youth resides in them more conspicuously even than in girls. It doesn't want to let them go, it clings to them, it cherishes them, and its lingering presence, like the last light of evening, strikes me precisely for my not taking it for granted, as I might instead the light of midday, or youth in an eighteen-year-old. I like, too, the shadowy depths around the orbits, the expressive lines that branch from them, lines that tell more, I think, than a smooth round face.

I'm not interested in knowing how old they are. I would rather not know their age. Sometimes I resent it if someone tells me. I am all for people who make a mystery of it. Let doctors and passport officials ask the date of birth. I would rather live with my illusions: for me appearance is reality. For me they are ageless. And if, at times, despite myself, I do wonder about their age, or someone tiresomely insists I make a guess, I invariably and quite sincerely give them a low figure—judge them to be much younger than they are. Nor can I tell or do I ever ask myself if someone or other is wearing a wig, or if the hair is its natural color. That sort of speculation is alien to my mind, and I don't entertain it for a moment. I have no taste for birthdays, except those of children or of the very old—when age becomes a matter of pride.

One August day, when I was in my mid-thirties, Jeremy, an Englishman who was staying with a girlfriend and a couple in a cottage in the mountains, about twenty miles from my parents' home in the Tuscan countryside, and who knew that we took paying guests, telephoned to ask if we had a room for a friend of his called Claire who was coming to Italy from London. I told him that we had.

"She knows all about you," he said.

"Oh, dear," I said.

He laughed. "No," he said. "I mean, she's seen some of your sketches, and knows about the house."

About the house I suppose he meant the casual, rather artistic atmosphere prevailing there. As for my sketches, I had made a small name for myself with them, and some had been shown in London and New York.

"What is she like?" I said.

"Charming," he said. "You'll see."

She stepped out of the taxi blithely, one long leg and tapering foot after another, and lightly trod on the pebbles of the yard on high thin heels, crane-like. She didn't so much give me her hand as proffer it, and I wished I could hold it longer than I did. She was blond and tall and very slender, and to me she seemed younger than I—as young as the new moon, or a gold coin just minted. She had a born-yesterday look, an innocence, a pureness really, or better still, a limpidity about her that came straight through to me and which the years couldn't obscure. It showed through them, a light too luminous for them to eclipse. The turn of the years swathes most people with layers which little by little cover what greenness they have—the green core of freshness that is in us all. Well, in her that core was still extant, still quite apparent, and it refreshed me to look at her. Willowy she looked—supple as a willow. So willowy and supple I had an urge to bend her to me. Oh, she would give, yield unwillingly like those shoots the Tuscan farmers use to tie vines and train them onto stakes. A rough farmer I was, and she a soft nymph. She leaned toward me a little as I gave her my arm up the two steps to the front door. Near her, I felt as if in the shade of a fragrant tree, except that I felt warmth too, with the coolness. It was early afternoon, the sun blazing, the air outside hot and dry; the cicadas dinned. Inside, the house was relatively cool. But with the front door open, waves of heat were coming in as from a furnace. She had insisted on carrying a small bag herself. Halfway up the staircase, she paused and set it on the landing and sighed. I stopped too, beside her. She seemed a little faint, overcome by the heat, and tired from the long journey from England by plane, train, taxi. Like a professional porter, I put the little bag under my arm while the heavy one hung from my closed hand. My free hand I placed on the small of her back to lend her some support.

"That's nice," she said, lingering pleasantly on the *i* of the word "nice," and taking full advantage of my hand, resumed the climb.

We reached her room. I opened the outside shutters to let in the breeze and show her the view. The tall cypresses were swaying gently, rocking as someone might on a hammock on a lazy summer afternoon.

"I've seen those *before*," she said.

"Where?"

"In your sketches."

"Lawrence says something about cypresses being like flames of darkness that keep the night aglow during the day."

"They were *beautifully* drawn," she said, returning to me.

"I know them well. I used to hide in them as a boy, and with them sway to and fro. I wish we had done that together."

"I do too."

"Perhaps we are still in time," I said, and looked up at the gigantic trees.

"Yes," she said, and clenched my hand in a moment of excitement as if she were about ready to race to them. She sighed again. "No, I think I'll take a little *rest* now," she said, resting on the word "rest," looking at the bed, and making it seem most attractive. "But a little later do you think you could call a taxi for me? I'm supposed to go and see Jeremy."

"It's quite a long way," I said, "about twenty miles, over rough roads in part. I'll drive you there if you like."

"Would you really, but it's too *far*," she said in a voice modulated by the softest intonations. The word "far" in particular seemed to prolong itself infinitely, and gave me a wonderful feeling of distance.

"It's not *that* far," I said, "and with you not at all far."

"But really would you want to take me?"

"Yes, if you'll be nice to me."

"I'll be very nice to you."

She spoke slowly, in a way all her own, that no one could have taught her. As it happened I thought hers was the most beautiful English, but I think I would have liked it even if she had spoken Cockney. Her soul was in her voice, and it came soft and sweet as rain after a drought.

So we drove to the foothills of the mountains and then up the mountain to the cottage where Jeremy and his friends lived. I was going to leave her there, since they had a car and I thought they could drive her back. But it turned out they couldn't—they had a tennis appointment later on.

"Then I'd better wait for her," I said, aside, to Jeremy.

"Oh, she can take a taxi."

"It's an expensive ride."

"Oh, don't worry about that," he said with a gesture (he was an actor) which made it clear that it was nothing to her. He added that she was "the bonbon queen of England," heiress to some huge confectionery fortune, that in London they had a theater, that her husband directed plays and gambled and raced cars, all with her money.

The bonbon queen of England—when he said it I couldn't help thinking how well the title suited her. "Well, she's very sweet," I said.

"Very," he said, and took a sip of Scotch.

I was ready to go, especially since the other man of the house didn't seem to want me to remain. But rather touchingly she begged me to stay on. The place had been a farmhouse. Where there once had been a thrashing yard, now there was a swimming pool. They swam. I think she was glad of my company. Without me, there would have been three women and two men. But it was more than that. Though we had only met that day, I sensed that she felt closer to me than to them.

We returned home for dinner, which at that time of year we had out in the garden. The tourist season being at

to mock the years

its height, there was quite a number of us at the table—
at least twelve. She sat next to me. I held hands with her
between our chairs, unseen. Two other English ladies were
staying with us. There was no secret about their ages, poor
dears—they were and looked old, big, heavy and flabby,
with double chins and whitish curly hair. At a certain point
one of them looked down the table at her and cried,
"Claire!"

"Yes," she said.

"Claire, I'm Betty."

"Oh."

I felt her hand twitching, involuntarily.

"Claire, it's ages since I've seen you, but you look just
the same," she said, and turning to the rest of us, explained,
"We were at school together."

"Yes," she said softly.

"My goodness," the woman went on, and would have
pursued the conversation, but Claire was in no mood to;
she turned to me again, her hand held mine tighter, and
she changed the subject.

"Wasn't it funny," I said later, walking in the garden
with her after supper, "meeting that lady here?"

"Now you know my *age*," she said sadly.

"Was she your teacher?" I said.

She laughed, and, embracing her, I lifted her like a
child off the gravel path and twirled with her two or three
times.

I looked at her in the kind light of the moon. She
defied age. The years she vanquished. If I was fond of her
before, I loved her now.

solitude

He looked at the fireplace, about the only remarkable thing in the apartment. It was made of
the local stone—*peperino* (pepper-like)—that the
mason had told him was quarried nowhere else in
the world. He admired its mantel and sides, the
graceful curves they made. It was probably four
hundred years old, like the rest of the building and
most of the village. He wished he had a pair of
andirons, and again he regretted not having taken
the old ones from his family's house, now sold.
He had stupidly left them for the new owner.

Antiques, too. Never mind, he would have the plumber, who also worked wrought iron, make him a pair. Start anew.

When, last year, he had bought this apartment (through a classified ad) and had it completely restored, he had looked forward to this moment, in which everything would be finally in place and he would be sitting where he was, in a red velvet armchair. All I want, he had thought, is to light a fire and watch the flames. But now, after spending all day unpacking and putting things away, he felt too tired to do anything, and besides, it wasn't cold and he hadn't bought any logs. So he just gazed at the empty fireplace and poured himself a glass of wine. Then he thought of a cheap picture frame that had fallen apart and of a few slats of wood he didn't need, all of which he had piled up neatly under the sink. He picked them up, stacked them in the fireplace, put some paper under them, and lit them. The old wood caught fire easily. He watched them burn. Smoothly, without a crackle, the flames consumed them till they were a small, blackened little heap. It was hardly the fire he had envisaged, and if anything it made him sadder.

He looked around him and he thought: What folly, why am I here? What possessed me to buy this place? Why didn't I just send everything to America, home? Why did I need this? Be done with this old country. Just come as a tourist, not to stay. I haven't a friend in the whole village, not a friend within fifty miles. Yes, one, but this one had irritated him when—the place still unfinished—he had come to see it and all he had been able to say was that it was too noisy. Well, it was rather noisy, right in the center of the village, on the Piazza della Repubblica—as in many other Italian towns, the usual name for the main square—children playing outside the windows, men standing around and talking, cars and motorscooters starting up, but then in that man's house, out in the country, when he had been to see *him,* he had to put up with worse noises—a tractor roaring, dogs barking, the television blaring; and, right here, now, in the middle of the night, it was very quiet. He couldn't hear a sound, except, once in a while, that of the nightingales down a steep slope, amid the olive trees, and who would object to them?

He went out on the balcony, at the top of the outside stone staircase, also of *peperino*—everything here was built of *peperino*—and looked at the stars. They were supposed to be a comfort to the sight—the one thing that, along with flowers, a blind man who recovered his sight said he wasn't disappointed with. Other worlds spun around them. And this world was a mere speck compared to them. But though a dot he was compared to the world, and though a dot the world was to them, his state of mind would not be belittled—nor would an ant's, for that matter.

The clock on the gateway to the castle, now town hall, above the square, marked the wrong time, eleven o'clock, and it probably had for years. He re-entered the house, shut the door and went to his best window, the one that looked down into the steep valley and up again to the brow of a rocky cliff. It was all blackness, but to the left, in the distance, there was a cluster of lights, another cluster, beyond it, and another, and another—villages like this one, perched up high on the horizon.

Above them was the night sky with its haze of stars, not nearly so dark as the valley. In the daytime, looking in that direction, you could see the Apennines, still white with snow, some fifty miles off, and the cliff, less than a mile away, crowned by golden tufts of broom. He could hear the notes of the nightingales, some faint, some clear, depending on how far they were. The whole valley seemed to be singing.

Well, what's so bad about that, he thought, and turned, more content, to the interior and went to bed.

One sixth of the way around the globe, in Massachusetts where it was still daylight, his wife and three children must have had supper and were perhaps watching television, a tight-knit little group. He had come from America to finish fixing this place up. It was much too small for the whole family, but it would do as a *pied-à terre*. It was a good vantage point to view Central Italy from. Fifty miles north of Rome, in Etruscan country. A hundred miles south of Florence. Orvieto, Perugia, Viterbo within easy reach. Perhaps his children, when they grew up and got married, could use it for their honeymoon, he thought. Or he and his wife, who had never had a proper honeymoon, could come. Or he might just come here by himself once in a while, to have a rest, to be alone, as now.

He listened to the nightingales and, the light still on, he looked at the well scraped, dark-stained rafters and the clean bricks between them. The mason had done a good job. The apartment, with its outside staircase, its own roof, and no one below him, was almost as self-contained as a house. He might just stay on. Not return. But leave his wife and children, "those precious motives, those strong knots of love?"

The thought had crossed his mind before. He could continue his artwork here, or, since lately he had barely been able to support his family with it, he could turn his little studio into an office, a doctor's office. Twenty years before, here in Italy, in Rome, he had been a doctor, a physician. He had given up his practice, left medicine for art, a passion that had haunted him all through his medical days, and before that. Perhaps he should resume practicing, take some refresher courses, renew his license, and begin again, here, in this village. God, the thought gave him a heavy sinking feeling. He was so free the way he was. And medicine—the horror of making a mistake, the anxiety that went with it, the social intercourse, the weight of other people's troubles on his own. No, he could not go back to it. Something else maybe, but not that. There was a nice pottery in this village, buy some here and elsewhere in Italy, send a whole load of it to America, and sell it on the porch of his home on Main Street in Cape Cod—commerce, business. Easier to do that. No, again a sinking feeling. Pottery so heavy, baked clay, stone across the ocean. Stick to his present work, get up now and go to his desk, his pens, his pencils, the blank sheets of paper that became worthless at a touch, or sometimes—rarely, rarely—fairly valuable. It must be near dawn. He put the light out and looked at the window. No, it was still night. Bless the night. "Thou layest thy finger on the lips of Care, / And they complain no more."

He woke up to the voices of children going to school and to the revving up of the motors of people going to work. Then a lull. Midmorning. The children were in their classrooms, the adults in workshops and in fields. He lay in bed. Why get up? Why face another day? Because. He hardly knew why. Just because. The wonderful answer in Italian, "*Perchè sì.*"

He looked out his favorite window at the cliff wreathed in gold. Now *there* was a view. Not many views like that out of windows. He would explore the countryside. He liked to take walks, new walks, and here everything was new to him.

Outside, people looked at him—the stranger in town. He felt very self-conscious. Oh, to be in a big city, where no one knew, no one cared who you were. Why did they stare so, and how long would he be able to stand it? He passed by a tiny girl, three or four years old, standing next to an old man, probably her grandfather, sitting on a doorstep. "Who is that little man?" he heard her say. "Is he ugly?" Now why would she've said that? His unfamiliar look, his uncombed hair might have displeased her, but he wasn't small. On he went, down the main road. Very soon he was out of the village. Half a mile farther, he crossed the edge of the road into a field and felt safe from any glances. The open countryside had a universality about it that the village lacked. Like being on the sea or on a vast shore. Green all around him. A sea of green. And the song of the birds was universal, too. Or at least international.

solitude

They sang just this way in America, and in Asia. The same calls. Suddenly he felt very happy. The terrain was fertile and had, till not long ago, been intensely cultivated. Recently, however, with many of the farmers working in factories, it had been more or less left to itself and it looked like a half-abandoned garden. Unkempt. The ground under the vines and olive trees was unhoed. The grass grew high. Here and there it seemed to overwhelm the vines. He came to a cherry tree loaded with ripe cherries. Was no one going to pick them? He savored one and another and another, and then a handful. They quenched his thirst. Stolen fruit—twice as delicious. Soon he came to another tree, also unpicked. Some of the cherries, overripe, had fallen on the ground. People must be fairly well off, he thought, to let this bounty go. In stores he had bought them for a dollar a pound. These were better. Of all fruit, cherries were best when eaten off the tree. His lips were red with juice. Lipstick after a stolen kiss. One had a healed gash on it. A beak did that, he thought—a trill of the wings between leaves, between branches to keep still for a moment while the bill cut cleanly, picked at the pulp, then off like a thief, with the juice fresh in the mouth, in the throat, in the gullet, in the breast, in the body, to keep strong the wings, live the song.

Taking a zigzag path down the slope he wandered on, trying to reach a cluster of broom he was sure he had seen from the road. He had lost sight of it, but now, still unseen, yet close, its blossoms, courtesan-wise, announced themselves to him with their perfume. A heady scent. He grazed the string of cool, yellow blossoms with his face. He came to a cave, exposed to the sun, dry and inviting, larger than his apartment. People had probably lived here in prehistoric times. There were some rectangular niches dug into the walls. For pots and pans? "No," the mason, who knew quite a lot about the history of the place, told him later in a reverent tone of voice, "the Etruscans set urns there with the ashes of their dead." It was better to think of pots and pans and little dishes, flasks of wine and olive oil, and earthen jars of various jams and honey. Knowledge was so often sad. Once, in Rome, as a child, overjoyed to see four horses pulling a coach bedecked with flowers, he had asked his mother if he could ride on it. "But, darling," she answered, "that's a hearse." These lush slopes were of volcanic origin. Mount Cimino, the extinct volcano, dominated the landscape to the west. It was a wooded mountain with a growth of taller trees—colossal, ancestral beeches—on its peak. Ages ago, flames erupted from it, and now these cool trees soughed in the wind. The village water also came from there. It in fact supplied the water of all the towns around it. Extinct volcanoes were apparently full of surprises. Not just water—ores, all kinds of things. In ancient days, until a Roman consul crossed it, the forest on the mountain was famed for being impassable, and though now a road led to the top, it still looked awesome.

Each day he went for longer walks, till it seemed to him he was regaining the vigor of his youth when mountain climbing had been one of his pleasures. Down ravines he went, across streams, up precipices made bare by torrential rains, from foothold to foothold, nook to nook, pausing to catch his breath on a ledge once in a while. Precariously balanced on a rock, he viewed the chasm below with wonder and the height above with such a sense of expectation that his body felt in turn molten and tense. Ready and poised for more, he would focus on the next step only. Sometimes—bridging a gap or skirting a passage where the ground crumbled at his feet—it was only speed, momentum that kept him from falling, and then there was no stopping. Soon he had reached the top, and there he took a rest that was the reward of the climb, worth all the effort, a rest full of satisfaction, especially when he considered the enormous detour he would have had to take had he not come by this short cut, for the stream at the bottom of the narrow gorge went on for miles.

The wilderness had reclaimed some of the paths and they were hard to follow. Yet here and there he came to signs which told this was an ancient land, well tilled and tended. From a row of flat stones that bore the mark of rims he surmised that what was now a path might once have been a road. A colossal rock beneath a cliff had a still inhabitable lean-to, made of stone. On a ridge he came to a wall—large blocks of stone set one upon the other without mortar and at one end the stub of an arch, as he deduced from a few half-buried wedge-like stones. Farther on there was a slab, perhaps marking a grave. Etruscan? Their houses were of wood. All there was left of their towns were the walls around them, the paving stones, the sculpture and the tombs. Where he trod a city might have flourished.

Again and again he came to cherry trees with cherries ripe and lush and once, even more thirst-quenching, to a medlar. In one of his walks he took a trail that led to a field of hazels. The nuts were tiny in this season, for they ripened and were gathered in September. On and on he went, from one field to another, till he had covered three or four miles. The hazels were planted in rows on the slopes of hills, wherever the terrain would permit, down to the stream and up to the edge of the rocky cliffs. He got quite thirsty. There were no cherry trees or medlars here. High on a slope he heard a gurgling sound, and there, by the side of the track he followed, was a spring, clear and abundant. He knelt on the ground and stooped, stretched his neck down like a camel to reach the water and drank. It was very cold, coming as it did from the deep, dark, secret, underground veins of the tall, wooded hill. Fresh and very cold, testifying to its pureness, to its freshness. He drew the water in, and paused, and rose as drinking camels do, and then went down again for a second draft to slake all of his thirst.

And through his walks he got to know and love this land of cliffs and brows of hills and deep-set streams. Amid the luxuriant vegetation he didn't feel alone. Only, at times, he wished he could share the smells and sights and sounds with someone else. It seemed a shame, a waste that he should have all that beauty to himself. But in the studio he did feel very much alone, so alone he struck up imaginary conversations with his wife and younger daughter, Silvia, conversations such as he might have on his return home, to America. The dialogue ran like this:

Wife: But it was madness to buy it.
He: Silvia, outside you can hear clop-clop, cloppety-clop, and it's a donkey with an old man sitting on it, bundles of grass on each side, and another donkey following close behind with just a load of grass.
Wife: How could you think of buying such a place? Too small for us. And noisy, you say. Under everyone's eyes.
He: Once, Silvia, I was sitting in my armchair and who came to the window but a pigeon. And perched on a roof top, there's an owl almost every night, in the same spot. So still that for a while I thought it was made of stone.

Indirect reply, he thought. A new technique. Avoids argument.

But soon he came back to himself and to the present.

He had been there three weeks and had got no mail, though he had written home twice. Then one day, returning from a long walk, he found a letter slipped under his door, a letter from a friend in New York. In three weeks she was coming to Italy, she said, and could they meet. She spoke tenderly, and he was touched, moved, and as expectant as he had been on the face of the cliff when his pulse quickened and he got a molten feeling in his midriff. His plane left in fifteen days, nor could he cancel his

solitude

85

reservation and make a new one without losing a good deal of money. What's more, his wife was expecting him back on the set date, and, in three weeks, he was supposed to start teaching once a week at a summer school. Why, why had he got himself into that? He reread the letter, saw the girl—blonde, sleek, smiling, promising all the joys he had missed. The two of them here. Just right for two, this place. The villagers who looked at him rather pitifully would look at him in a very different way with her around—the women with surprise, the men with envy, especially those loud-mouthed boys on their hideous motorcycles. Damn it. He could send a telegram to the school, "Return delayed, sorry," or make up an excuse, lie. "Sick." No, that might worry his wife and induce her to fly over, turn up at the most awkward time. Just, "Return delayed," to both—to wife and school—and to the girl, "Hurry, waiting," or something of the sort, plus a long letter. He pictured her with him under the cherry trees, under the medlar tree, by the broom blossoms, by the spring, and here in bed. Best of all here in bed, in this studio or apartment that so much needed someone else, that was so sterile and stark without a woman, that smelled only of tobacco and books. A whiff of perfume, her perfume. He could sense it. Spend the whole summer here, never return, cancel the ticket back, stay on and on.

He did nothing. Slowly, as the days went by, the effect of the letter seemed to wane; like pain the delicious pleasure of her imagined presence waned. He wrote the girl to try and come sooner, but she didn't. He heard from her no more.

An old man, at least twenty years older than he was began to talk to him and treat him as if he were his age, nearly seventy. He even went as far as saying, "Stay on, two little old men, we'll keep each other company in the winter." Good God, he felt a terrifying urge to leave, to flee, to fly. There was America, with his wife, his children, his house, the summer school, the women students whom he

solitude

didn't know and two whom he knew, a whole lot of people waiting for him, life teeming, life to take and to hold, precious, strong, coming to him like a river. Not this trickle. He felt an urge to go out to the nearest phone and call TWA to change his reservation to tomorrow. But that urge, too, subsided. No, he would just wait for the set day. It would come soon now, in only another week.

dante

You know how it is with people who've been alone for a long time, they start talking to anything, even to themselves. Well, I'd been alone for months, without even a cat to talk to, up on the top floor of a tall elevatorless building on Piazza Santa Croce in Florence. The apartment had a terrace, and I would spend hours there looking at the view. In the foreground, right in the middle of the square, there was a marble statue of Dante, which now has been shifted to a corner of the square. Wisely, I think—the statue isn't great, except in size. It has a brooding look. At times it seemed to be frowning at me. It didn't at all fit the picture I had formed of him from his poetry. I imagined him pensive, perhaps even suffering— bereft of Beatrice and an exile as he was—but definitely not frowning. No sneer of cold command, no haughty *condottottiere* look as in Verrocchio's Colleoni in Venice, but rather a man who easily fell in love, sensitive, compassionate, very gentle. And this conception of him was confirmed by Giotto's frescoed figure of him in the Bargello: that profile has a delicate, almost speaking mouth, and a serene quality which I couldn't see in Enrico Pazzi's statue there before me. So I was fairly disturbed each time I looked at it. But in a way he was company, and alone and lonely as I was, one day I started talking to him, the poet absent and yet present.

"That's meant to be a portrait of you, Dante, my dear man, but it's in fact a misrepresentation, a lie," I said, sotto voce. "It's not like you at all. You who spoke so tenderly to Francesca are just not there. You who loved her with her love, a love that the fire of hell could not consume, a love that triumphed even over a condemning God, could never look like that. You know, they put this statue up 600 years after your birth to commemorate you, and to make up for your not being buried there in Santa Croce, along with other great Italians, like Michelangelo and Galileo. The Florentines, who banished you, tried to get you back here after you died and became famous, but the people of Ravenna, who sheltered you, wouldn't let go of you. And I don't blame them. I don't think you blame them either. You probably want to rest in peace there where they laid you. The Florentines ought to've loved you in your lifetime, not after death. They have no claim. You've been in hell, purgatory and paradise. You know those places as well as any could. And not just those places, also the people there, talked to them, suffered and rejoiced with them, shared their sorrows and their joys. You who returned to us from a journey of no return, returned to us from the world of the hereafter, you alone of mortals to've visited those places and come back, I shouldn't think you'd want to undertake another journey in this world which you've already seen and seen so well, which you've so fully explored. Past. Past. The new you sought, in spheres beyond our ken. There's nowhere left to go, there's nowhere right. Might as well just rest, there in Ravenna, in the darkness of the tomb, where night is never cleared by dawn or other light."

I felt impossibly close to him as I spoke, felt in communion with him. Many other people in the world must at that very moment have been thinking and writing about or reading Dante, but was anyone else speaking to him?

When I ceased, I went indoors from the terrace and lay down. I fell asleep and dreamed and there he was, Dante, right in front of me, not cold and hard and statued, but as someone who wanted to hear more. There he was indeed, with a courteous look about him and an inquisitive, subtle, pleasant air—the welcome visitor, the sublime reporter, the interviewer par excellence.

Yes, he seemed very live and real, as real as in the *Divine Comedy,* in which he talked to people not as in a dream. He was wearing a light hood, chin strap and cape, as in Giotto's fresco, and he looked familiar, looked just as I imagined him from reading his poetry.

"Dante!" I said, beside myself with excitement and surprise, and not a little embarrassed at the thought that I might have summoned him with my idle talk about his needing rest.

"Yes," he said, very meek and modest, "how did you know?"

"How did I know? You are famous. They call you the father of the nation."

"Me, the father of the nation?"

"Yes, look," I said, pointing out the window, "there's a statue of you, a monument to you, right in the middle of the square, here in Piazza Santa Croce."

"Yes, I know where I am. Though it's changed, I recognize this piazza well enough. I used to play around here as a child. But that statue, me?"

"It doesn't look like you, it's true, but it was meant to. It doesn't even have your nose, which is much more subtle."

"Thank you," he said. He laughed. "The father of the nation!"

"Yes, look," I said, and quickly drew out of my wallet a bank note, one of those that Italians playfully called "*tovaglie*"—tablecloths—because they were so large, and which now have been withdrawn from circulation. "Here's your picture. That's you well enough, isn't it? You recognize yourself? It's Giotto's portrait of you in the Bargello."

"Yes, that is me. But why am I there?"

"It's money. Oh, of course, you had coins, no paper money in those days. But it's legal tender all right."

He smiled. "Me on money! But not in gold."

"We don't use gold coins anymore, but if we did, you'd be on them, I assure you."

"Giotto's portrait of me, imagine. I knew Giotto."

"I know you did. '*Credette Cimabue nella pittura / Tener lo campo, ed ora ha Giotto il grido.*' Cimabue thought to hold the field in painting, and now Giotto is all the rage."

"You quote me right. Then you've read the *Commedia*?"

"They call it the *Divina Commedia* now. Of course I've read it, from beginning to end and more than once. No other Italian book has been so read."

"You don't say?"

"Look, I have it." And I showed him a copy.

He fingered the pages with amusement. "So they've come to see the light. But the father of the nation! I didn't found anything."

"You think you didn't, but you did. Ah, you are so nice and modest, as a poet should be, not pretentious, like some of the modern ones. Why, the Italian language has its foundations in you. You are considered our greatest poet, our greatest man."

He laughed incredulously, pleased and surprised, but also as if I were trying to fool him. "Greater than Virgil?"

"Yes, greater than he."

"Greater than Saint Francis?"

"Yes, greater, sure, greater, I would say."

"Hush! Don't be heard saying things like that. It's sacrilege." But he proceeded playfully, as in a game. "Greater than the popes?"

"Oh, the popes! Of course greater than they."

"And the kings and emperors?"

"Much greater than they. They are half forgotten. They are nothing to you."

He drew his arms back and looked up and laughed. "You know, in the *Comedy* I explored the past, and now I've come back on earth to find out what happened since I left it, the future so to speak. What happened?"

"What hasn't? You've grown in stature, while we have become smaller."

He shrugged his shoulders with impatience, revealing a different side of his character. "Let's talk no more about me," he said, "all this adulation is suspect. If you are trying to curry favor you came to the wrong man. I have no influence. None whatever. I am a banished man."

"No influence! You the most influential Italian of them all."

"Enough of that. I was an ambassador for a while, to San Gimignano. But I was banished. I became an exile and wandered from land to land, from place to place, ended in Ravenna."

"I know that."

"You do?"

"Of course, but don't worry. I'm not asking for favors. It's the greatest favor just to be able to talk to you, hear you, see you."

dante

93

"Tell me, what happened to Florence?"

"It's full of tourists."

"Tourists? What are tourists?"

"People who come to see the sights, even the house you lived in, and all the other wonders of this town."

"And the world? What's happened to the world?"

"They discovered America, a new land to the west, just as you foretold."

"Oh, you read that? In my Ulysses canto."

"Yes. It was discovered by a man called Columbus, from our shores. And man has been to the moon."

"The moon?"

"Yes, but in your book you went there and also to the stars. We haven't got to the stars yet."

"And Italy?"

"Is united now."

"Strong?"

"Not so very. The world is round. There are so many nations. Some much larger."

"I don't doubt it."

"There've been wars that make those of your time seem puny besides."

"God help you."

"We drive in cars, sail in ships, and fly in airplanes all with fiery engines, and we have drugs to cure us of most ills."

"But you still die?"

"Oh yes, we die."

"And love?"

"We love. Whatever else may be said of this world, this can't be denied: we still do love."

"That's the main thing. Then there is hope. Bless the Earth—it may be the only place where love gives birth."

This was a rhyme worthy of the poet, and proved his presence—that he was no fraud, no impersonator or impostor, no figment of my imagination either—I couldn't have thought it up, not even in a dream.

"Do you think I would be happy living here?" he asked.
"Not without Beatrice."

"She's in heaven. And now I must leave. Good-bye," he said.

He disappeared. I awoke and light put out the light. The voice was silent and the image fled. Then like a faithful scribe I wrote all down.

the italian class

About my age, suffice it to say that the last woman who invited me to dinner gave me a choice of left-overs, and as for my wife, if I ask her a question, half the time she doesn't bother to reply. My letters, too, often go unanswered, and what little I manage to write is rejected. Not like in the old days, when newsstands and bookstores often carried something I'd written, and in the subway I saw a young woman reading a short story of mine in a magazine open on her lap. I could make a living from my writing then. Not anymore. I feel like a baker whose bread nobody buys. After a while you give up. New tastes. Old age is descending on me like a hood, benighting me.

"Come to terms with it," I tell myself. And I must say there is some comfort in this thought. Peace. The struggle is over. Sit back and contemplate. From contemplation at least no one can stop me. It is a perfectly harmless pursuit. Though perhaps pursuit isn't the right word. Just a pastime—while your time away in contemplation. The sea, the sky, the lay of the land.

Suddenly, momentarily, everything is acceptable to me, even serene. I go out into the front yard and to my delight hear a mourning dove. No voice could be more welcome. Soft, mellow, and far from mournful. Harbinger of spring. Messenger of love. Ubiquitous.

And I say to myself, why publish or write? Why try to make a work of art of words, notes, colors, or clay? Why not try to make a work of art of your own life? Living is the important thing—being rather than doing. To do or not to do isn't the question. Yet doing is part of living, nor does one want an empty life.

And so, sitting in an armchair, my eyes wander to the want ads of the local newspaper. Now, who would want me at my age? I look under 'instruction' and find to my surprise that the Adult Education Program needs language teachers. I can teach my native language, Italian, which I taught, along with literature and creative writing, until two years ago when I retired. I try the number and a woman answers. With no questions asked other than which day of the week would suit me, she takes me on, for ten weeks, Tuesday evenings, from seven to nine, starting the week after next. So there I am with a job again. Easier than I thought. And I'm glad, for I do miss students—their intent look, their receptive stance.

They are adults, except for one, a nine-year-old, who comes with his father and, unlike his father, pronounces the words after me with a perfect accent. Wonderful this faculty that children have. There is a woman who is here because she is a singer. Two are going to Italy soon on a group vacation. And there is a woman who wants to refresh her knowledge of the Italian that she learned long ago when she spent a year in Tuscany.

I pretend we are about to board a plane to Italy. Soon we are in Rome, at the airport, the metro, the station, in a taxi, at a hotel, a store, at a restaurant. And for a moment I'm with them; with words and gestures I do my best to transport them there, and their pleasure is my pleasure; through their eyes it's as if I were in Rome for the first time. Their anticipation becomes mine. We walk along my favorite streets, hear the gurgle of a fountain or feel its spray. We have coffee at the Caffè Greco. We climb the Spanish Steps.

When I return home, as from a long journey, there is a good smell of cooking in the kitchen. Though it's around 9:30, my wife has waited for me. She certainly is a good cook. And where did I read that a man isn't likely to leave his wife if she cooks well? This morning, when I got up, I found four cupcakes with lemon icing on the kitchen table. They look like flowers. Her cooking—it's her way of showing her love for me now.

I feel less isolated teaching, but so far I haven't really made friends with any of the students. After class we each go our separate ways. The singer did say something about meeting at her place some evening. Did she mean after class? But she never mentioned it again. She has a winning smile. It is so sincere you feel she may have a predilection for you. Her hair is cut very very short. She has a spare, lean look, a finely graven face. She sings in English, French, German, sophisticated café-chantant songs. She hopes to add some Italian ones to her repertoire. That's why she is here; a serious student. She sings for a living in various places, especially in the summer, when life quickens in this town. Naturally she is particularly interested in the pronunciation of the vowels. I am delighted with her efforts. I don't mind telling the class that I was born in Rome and grew up in Siena, a combination that is supposed to make for the best accent. She smiles appreciatively. I go over some of the musical directions, such as *'allegro,'* and *'andante,'* and *'con brio,'* and tell her (and the rest of the class) that I wish I knew more of them. The next time we meet, bless her, she brings me a complete list of them. This class is in danger of becoming a duet, and to include them all I go back to the old routines, hotel, restaurant shop-talk. But, how dull it is, compared to music. As if sensing an anticlimax, she asks me, "How do you say, 'I love you'?"

"*Ti amo,*" I reply, "or, more commonly, *"Ti voglio bene, ti voglio tanto bene."* And I am reminded of a song that Beniamino Gigli used to sing, beginning with those words, which I try to repeat in my best tenor voice. I can't help looking at her as I sing. Again I try to include the rest of the class.

"Let's go through words of greeting, in conversation and in letters." And I go over various forms of well wishing, asking each one to repeat a phrase in turn. I tell them that Italians tend to be very affectionate in their letters to close relatives and friends or anyone they love and often say, *'Tanti baci'* (many kisses) and *'un abbraccio'* (a hug), at the end. From there, I go into the language of love and its uneven terrain. I ask one of them to say, "*Accarezzami*" (caress me) and to another, "*Dammi un bacio*" (give me a kiss). I happen to say that to the wife in the class, whose turn it is. I don't mean to ask her for a kiss, of course, but I can see that she is a little peeved by my request. She is an attractive, buxom woman. Her husband, a good-looking man, is beside her. She would obviously never ask me, an old professor, for a kiss, and she hesitates. I repeat the phrase, as if she hasn't understood it, though I know she has, and finally, she says it. "*Bene,*" I say (good).

We travel back onto charted land—to Florence, Venice, Pisa, and I tell them of the notable things there, and about their artists, poets, and musicians. For them to practice reading and at the same time to learn better the rhythm of the language, I give them, each Tuesday, poems by a turn-of-the-century poet who uses plenty of easy dialogue.

As the weeks draw on, the class dwindles. The married couple hasn't shown up since I asked the wife to say "Give me a kiss," though I don't really think there's a connection. But the singer still comes, along with a few others. One day, she brings the scores for three Italian songs and we go over them in class but she won't sing them. "I need my accordion," she says. "In May, I'll give a concert, at the Art Association."

The next Tuesday, she's not there, and I miss her more than I can say. Two of the students have gone off to Italy on their two-week tour. Only the father and son are present, the boy way ahead of his dad.

On the Tuesday after that, there's no one in the classroom when I arrive, and I wander about the room looking at the posters, mainly French. By the back wall there is a bust of Dante, whom I immediately recognize by his distinctive nose and laurel wreath. Getting closer, I read his name on the pedestal.

To my delight the singer arrives. "We are not alone," I tell her. "There's Dante." And I show her the bust. I am well aware that she has a higher gift for languages than the others. In their absence, we go over some of Dante's verses that I know by heart and write them on the blackboard. How well she reads, and how clear her voice is. The poet himself would, I am sure, have liked to hear her. His words in her voice. And I wonder about her and I wish I knew her better, more and more intimately. And I remember what she said about going over to her house sometime. She never did bring it up again.

The next time I go to the classroom there's absolutely no one there. I wait and wait, but no one comes. On my way out I meet the janitor in the hall. "No one came," I tell him.

"It happens in the other classes too," he says as if to console me. He's a nice old fellow (I expect a good deal younger than I am).

Leaving the school, the thought of the empty classroom gives me a hollow feeling that leads to self-doubt, relieved only by disdain. If they want to learn, it is their loss. I drive to the beach. The sun has set, but diffuse fields of fast-fading violets and roses linger in the sky.

Home, I tell my wife, "No one came tonight."

"No one?"

"Not one."

"The course is called 'Conversational Italian.' Do you teach them that? What to say in stores and other places?" I can see she is wondering about my teaching.

"Yes, we do that, and some poetry."

"Poetry?"

"I give them poems with dialogue." Then I tell her what I said to the man's wife, and she, a Puritan soul, disapproves.

"I didn't think there was anything wrong."

"You'd better be careful here talking about kissing, in a class."

A week goes by and it is Tuesday again. She's there, the singer. And the young woman who went to Italy on a tour is back and present. She gives me a gift, a tiny address book from Florence with a picture of Pinocchio, about whom we had read a few pages in class.

She tells us about the cities she has seen. It is the end of April. We have only one more class left.

"I'm sorry but next Tuesday I won't be able to come," the singer says.

On Tuesday, the young woman who gave me the address book is the only one there.

"You are very faithful," I tell her.

"I thought that since this is the last day of class some of the others would come and we would have a little party, so I brought a fruit cake I bought in Siena, your home town."

"Oh, a *panforte!* My favorite," I say as she unwraps it.

She cuts a wedge for me and one for herself.

"Hm, it's exquisite, *squisito,*" I say.

"*Squisito,*" she repeats.

How nice she is. We converse till nine o'clock, in Italian as much as possible. She is originally from Connecticut, and she works at the town hall of a nearby town as an accountant. No errors in her books, I'm pretty sure. My last class and my last pupil, because I don't suppose I'll ever teach again, though this has been pleasant. She asks me if I'll be going to the singer's concert at the Art Association.

"Yes," I reply, and then I accompany her to her car where we meekly kiss good-bye.

The days fly by and the long-awaited concert is at hand. I arrive at the Art Association in good time. In loose, silken pants and matching blouse, an accordion strapped to her shoulders, she walks onto the stage, looks at us with her radiant smile, says a few words, then she ventures into song like a sweet bird taking to the air. French, that very sensual language, has never seemed so sensual to me as now. Rich and unencumbered flows her voice, filling the hall profusely, fresh and buoyant. The stream that issues from her inmost soul, a stream of joy, lilting and leaping like a rivulet, bathes, reaches my dry, my thirsty, barren being, until it seems to flourish with her song. And, there on the stage, she looks larger than life. In the classroom, sitting at her desk, like a schoolgirl, she seemed thin and small; now she looms tall, statuesque, and far more beautiful than I have ever seen her. Like a poet rapt in thought, till his physical being is almost transcended, she, borne by her song, looks like an angel. And not I alone feel this—

the italian class

everyone there seems to feel it, judging from the applause that crowns the ending. Again and again she soars in song, to heights unheard, unprecedented, or so they seem to me. Deep in my heart I am wild with commotion and surprise, and she and her singing, all in one, seem verily beautiful to me. I can hardly call myself a judge of songs—my musical education was sadly neglected—but never for a moment do I doubt the value of what I hear.

Later, at the concert's end, I go over to her to thank her, and gently, almost afraid, I return her kiss, and for a second, my hand rests on her and I feel her vibrant being, so very alive, the clothes between my fingers and her waist making her naked self even more real.

She would sing again, later in the season, at the Universalist Church, on Monday evenings. Would I, uncultured as I am, become one of those devotees who follow their favorite singer from theater to theater, town to town, considering everything else a waste of time?

The man who went to Italy on the group tour and didn't return to class, calls me to ask me if I would be willing to give a reading at the library. I tell him I will think about it and after some hesitation, I accept.

She comes to hear me, and at the end of the reading there is another kiss. After she leaves, I tell the man who invited me how I loved her concert and he says that she was singing as she left the library. "She's a *spirito canoro* (a melodious soul)," I say to him.

Summer begins and comes the night of her first concert in the church. I arrive a little late, wondering, can the triumph be repeated? Can she be as good as the first time? How can she, possibly?

If anything, she surpasses herself. Again, the joy, again the full, the sensual, the rich tones, coupled with her smile. She makes the bleak church basement seem like a café. I quite forget the place. I might be in Paris, in Montmartre, or on the Seine, with her voice, her song, matching the river's flow. And for a final number, telling the audience that this is for me, she sings an Italian song. And I bask in the bay of Naples with her, as on the wings of her song. It is a precious gift, this Italian song that she sings for me. I couldn't ask for more. I am touched, moved, delighted. A harvest such as this makes my teaching seem very worthwhile. Later, I thank her, and once again I kiss her, and feel again her vehement soul, the body of her soul between my palms. And then I leave.

I am not one to pursue. I have no will. A heavy weight of years has clipped my wings. But Mondays do return, the summer is still young, and I know where to find her.

escapes

He works and sleeps in his studio, across the backyard from the house, but, restless, he goes into the house again and again.

The movement helps, for stillness seems to increase a feeling of drifting. In the kitchen he switches on a burner under the half-filled aluminum coffee pot, then goes to sit on a rocking chair. It is one that he has recently mended—put new rockers on it, glued in a loose rung, pegged another, painted it all sage-green, and with the help of his daughter made new pillow slips for it. His sitting on it in comfort crowns the job, and for a moment he is on a throne. The coffee pot begins to groan. He fills a cup, resumes sitting and sips. Once in a while he rocks gently, and all the time he is groping for ideas—something, someone that will give him the energy to return to his studio, his desk, and his blank sheet of paper.

His wife comes into the kitchen. She seems quite content. Their elder daughter, nineteen, is living with her boyfriend in a neighboring town where they both have summer jobs; the younger daughter, fifteen, is for once reading in her room; their little boy, twelve, is down at the playing field at "recreation"—a town-financed program—and a certain stock has at last lost two points after climbing five since she sold it a week ago. Also, the yard, which during the winter and most of the spring looked so drab it seemed it could never be green or flourish again, pleases her now. She sees his despondent mood. "Do you want me to take you to a place you'll like?" she says, her green eyes bright and smiling, as if she had a great surprise in store for him.

"Where?" he says, bluntly. It is a question he shouldn't ask. He knows that no one likes to reveal a surprise right away, and knows how fond she is of surprises, whether they are for herself or for others. When they lived in New York, he remembers, she always wanted to go to theaters with sneak previews, no matter how dull the first movie was, and he knows how eager she is to unwrap any parcel. But still he looks at her as if expecting an answer—he has become rather skeptical in his middle age. What place can there possibly be that he hasn't seen in this village? They are on a strip of land only four miles wide, bounded by the ocean on one side and by the bay on the other. They have lived here nearly twenty years. He thinks he has driven or walked everywhere. And again, since she doesn't reply, he asks, "Where?"

"I went there a few days ago."

"Where is it?"

He sits as if nothing short of a wonder will budge him; so she says, "Past the dike and up the stream a bit, on a hill back of Duck Harbor."

"I've been there."

"You have? A place where there used to be a house?"

"A house? Well, all right, let's go there."

"Wait till you see it!" she says, confident now that he hasn't seen it.

They go to their big old open blue car and she drives. When they first came here she didn't know how, but he taught her, and now she does most of the driving. He feels like an old passenger. They cross the dike and then turn right onto an unpaved road along the stream, then left on a steep little road at the foot of a hill, and park the car there. They walk up the road between oaks and pines.

"One could even drive," she says.

"Not without losing the antenna."

"You can see it led to a house. Someone once told me there was one. I can't remember who."

"Clyde?"

"Yes, it must have been him."

Clyde, dead ten years now, was an old man who would often come by their house and tell them stories and things about the town that most, if not all, had forgotten. At his funeral he remembered her saying to Clyde's son, "We'll miss your father," in a voice so heartfelt it was touching.

She walks ahead of him fast.

"Slow down," he says. But she doesn't, and seeing her dappled by sunlight he's attracted and catches up with her and takes her bare arm in his.

"What are you doing?" she says playfully. "We are separated."

"By what?"

The back yard that is in between his studio and the house where she and the children sleep? His unfaithfulness? He's not one to select one person, and all the rest—

no matter how attractive—neglect. Time? They've been married twenty years and the bond has slackened almost to the point of being undone, though he tries to tighten it every once in a while.

"Let go."

"Let's find us a lair in the woods."

"Oh yeah?"

Her bare arm in his feels fresh and smooth, but she slides it away and again leaves him behind. He follows his guide.

"Have you been here before?" she asks him.

"No, maybe not." He's climbed this hill, but not along this road. "How far is it?"

"It's not far."

The road now is grassy and untrampled, unwalked other than by such creatures as will find a way between each stem. To him it's virgin, so are an untrodden snowy sidewalk, the wave-washed sand, the tide-swept beach, the wimpled wind-waved dune, the rippled lake—unplied except by ducks—and her clear, unruffled face. Not one stem is bent or broken. They come to the top of the hill and still the road continues, down a little, up some, level now, narrowing as it goes, overgrown with herbage bridged by branches.

"Here it is," she says.

He looks around him but sees no trace of a house. If anything, the wood seems thicker here. "How can you tell there was a house?"

"You see those lilacs there? They always planted lilacs in their yards."

They leave the road and walk toward the lilacs. Their blooming is over but still the flowers, turned brown, hang on. There is a pit, filled in with earth, strewn with leaves and flecked with plaster. He sees part of a brick. How long, how many springs have come and gone, since a family lived here, he wonders and he asks her.

"Old maps would tell," she says.

"Forty, fifty years?"

"Less, I think. In the winter, when the ground is bare, we'd be able to see more."

"We must come back. I suppose it was a farm."

"Yes."

"What did they grow? Corn?"

"Corn, potatoes. All sorts of root vegetables. And they had cows and sheep."

"It must have been all clear, with no woods."

"Oh, they kept part of their farm wooded, for their firewood."

He laughs. "You sound as though you saw it all happen."

All around them are some flowers, not quite out, which she tells him are day lilies. "They'll be out in a few days. Each blossom on each stem blooms for one day only. Look at them all. They are another sign there was a house. They escaped."

"Escaped?"

"Yes, they were cultivated and ran wild."

Again he laughs, delighted. She is a New England girl, was born across the bay, not like him who was born across the ocean.

"And look at the wild roses," she says, pointing down a hollow, speckled white. "I don't think I've ever seen so many."

"What are these?" he says, looking at some flowers at his feet.

"Celandine."

"That's a pretty name."

"Shelley used it. We have some in our backyard along the fence."

"And this?" he asks her, touching a cluster of white blossoms on a bough.

"Those are locust blossoms."

He smells them. They have a heady fragrance.

"The locust is another tree they liked to have around. It gets its leaves late and loses them early, so it didn't shade them in the cold. And it doesn't have pitch, so it's good for firewood, won't get the chimney as sooty as pine will. The locust is one more sign there was a house. Lilacs, daylilies, and locusts—they are three sure signs."

"You know so much," he says. "I wonder why they left."

"It got to be too out of the way after Duck Harbor was silted up and they dredged a new harbor in town."

"Perhaps they moved the house."

"No, it's too far up and down the hill. It was probably burned after they left."

"Were they able to make a living from farming?"

"No, they weren't just farmers; they also fished, and worked as handymen around town."

Slowly they walk back to the car. Driving home by a different route, along a marsh, she suddenly brakes to a stop. "Look," she says, pointing at a bush.

He notices nothing unusual for a moment, then in the brown intricacy of the branches sees an intensity of orange in the form of a little bird that flits from twig to twig and seems to find ample spaces in the thicket.

"An oriole," she says.

"A Baltimore oriole?"

"Yes, there's also the orchard oriole around here, smaller and a rich chestnut brown. We had one in our yard."

Back in his studio he is adrift again, lying on his bed and looking at the ceiling. Then he sees the house. There are no woods around it, except for a wooded lot and the locusts and lilacs. The corn is waving in the wind, and west, over the open fields, you can see the bay and the boats floating at anchor at Duck Harbor. The yard is aglow with daylilies. A brick chimney buttresses one side of the house. Outside the front door there's a slim-waisted girl with chestnut hair. She looks very much like his wife when he first saw her. No—she *is* his wife. Her neck is supple, her eyes very green, and there's something indomitable about her. She sees him coming up the road to the house. "Who is this stranger?" her eyes seem to be saying. "He must have taken the wrong turn somewhere."

How many wrong turns, he wonders. Should they have married? She surely belongs to this place, but does he? Shouldn't she have married someone whose step is light, who besides farming has a fishing boat and does odd jobs in the village? Someone with no drift to his life—whose life does not lack direction but holds a steady course, and who doesn't use tools to steady him but to further him on his way. Someone who doesn't search for a motif, and who, when the time to move into town shall have come, without a qualm will abandon the farmhouse where only the flowers will endure—the daylilies, the roses, the lilacs, and several locusts. The other things—the sills, the girders, the rafters—will all turn into ashes or dust. The plows, the hoes, the shovels and spades will all turn into rust.

He leaves the studio and goes into the kitchen. "That was a beautiful place," he says.

"Yes."

"Do you wish you'd married someone from around there?"

"There's no one around there."

"I mean someone like someone who might have lived there."

"No."

"You knew so much about it; it's as though you came from there. You are like a daylily who escaped across the bay."

"And what are you?"

"I don't know; thistledown, perhaps, that has escaped across the ocean and finds no rest anywhere for very long."

can-can

"I'm going to go for a drive," he said to his wife. "I'll be back in an hour or two."

He didn't often leave the house for more than the few minutes it took him to go to the post office or to a store, but spent his time hanging around, doing odd jobs—Mr Fix-it, his wife called him—and also, though not nearly enough of it, painting—which he made his living from.

"All right," his wife said brightly, as though he were doing her a favor. As the matter of fact, she didn't really like him to leave; she felt safer with him at home, and he helped looking after the children, especially the baby.

"You're glad to be rid of me, aren't you?" he said.

"Uh-huh," she said with a smile that suddenly made her look very pretty—someone to be missed.

She didn't ask him where he was going for his drive. She wasn't the least bit inquisitive, though jealous she was in silent, subtle ways.

As he put his coat on, he watched her. She was in the living room with their elder daughter. "Do the can-can, mother," the child said, at which she held up her skirt and did the can-can, kicking her legs up high in his direction.

He wasn't simply going out for a drive, as he had said, but going to a café, meet Sarah, whom his wife knew but did not suspect, and with her go to a house on a lake his wife knew nothing about—a summer cottage to which he had the key.

"Well, goodbye," he said.

"Bye," she called back, still dancing.

This wasn't the way a husband expected his wife— whom he was about to leave at home to go to another woman—to behave at all, he thought. He expected her to be sewing or washing, not doing the can-can, for God's sake. Yes, doing something uninteresting and unattractive, like darning children's clothes. She had no stockings on, no shoes, and her legs looked very white and smooth, secret, as though he had never touched them or come near them. Her feet, swinging up and down high in the air, seemed to be nodding to him. She held her skirt bunched up, attractively. Why was she doing that of all times *now*? He lingered. Her eyes had mockery in them, and she laughed. The child laughed with her as she danced. She was still dancing as he left the house.

He thought of the difficulties he had had arranging this *rendez-vous*—going out to a phone booth; phoning Sarah at her office (she was married, too); her being out; his calling her again; the busy signal; the coin falling out of sight, his opening the door of the phone booth in order to retrieve it; at last getting her on the line; her asking him to call again next week; finally setting a date.

Waiting for her at the café, he surprised himself hoping that she wouldn't come. The appointment was at three. It was now ten past. Well, she was often late. He looked at the clock, and at the picture window for her car. A car like hers and yet not hers—no luggage rack on it. The smooth hard-top gave him a peculiar pleasure. Why? It was 3.15 now. Perhaps she wouldn't come. No, if she was going to come at all, this was the most likely time for her to arrive. Twenty past. Ah, now there was some hope. Hope? How strange he should be hoping for her absence. Why had he made the appointment if he was hoping she would miss it? He didn't know why, but simpler, simpler if she didn't come. Because all he wanted now was to smoke that cigarette, drink that cup of coffee for the sake of them, and not to give himself something to do. And he wished he could go for a drive, free and easy, as he had said he would. But he waited, and at 3.30 she arrived. "I had almost given up hope," he said.

They drove to the house on the lake. As he held her in his arms he couldn't think of her; for the life of him he couldn't.

"What are you thinking about?" she said afterwards, sensing his detachment.

For a moment he didn't answer, then he said, "You really want to know what I was thinking of?"

"Yes," she said, a little anxiously.

He suppressed a laugh, as though what he was going to tell her was absurd or silly. "I was thinking of someone doing the can-can."

"Oh," she said, reassured. "For a moment I was afraid you were thinking of your wife."

the cricket

A cricket was chirping in the kitchen. Under the sink? Behind the stove? He could not tell. For a moment he even wondered if it weren't outside. No—the sound was too distinct for that. It was within. But where? The shrill, piercing note had a ubiquitous quality. It filled the room the way its companions outdoors filled the night. The only difference was that outside a choir was playing; this was a solo. And his only company. Playing for him. No—playing for itself, his presence absolutely irrelevant to it. It would chirp on if he left the kitchen and went upstairs to his bedroom. It wouldn't miss him. But he would miss it. Sometimes, for reasons unknown to him, it stopped, and the silence that followed soon became a tingling sound as the crickets outside took over. Or was it merely the tingling of the night, the night making "a weird sound of its own stillness"? Everything was so very still.

He had no radio, no television. To hear the news he sometimes went out to his car. He was alone in this house, one of several reserved for the faculty of the college where he had come to teach. He had been here three days. There were four other rooms, but so far no one else had shown up. Classes hadn't yet begun, that must be the reason. He was new and had come early, taking literally the college's recommendation to arrive right after Labor Day. The others, old hands, and most of them—from what he had heard—weekly commuters from New York, would wait. But any time now, someone would arrive, he was sure. Another day passed, however, and he was still alone. He and the cricket.

Outside, squirrels and chipmunks leapt from branch to branch, with a wavy motion and lightness that astounded him. At night, an owl hooted in the distance, more softly even than mourning doves cooed. Were he a bird, such a sound, he was certain, would be hard to resist. It was too entrancing, tempting, seducing; he would move and betray his presence, his whereabouts. Early in the morning, flickers would peck at the shingled walls of the house and wake him more effectively than an alarm clock. The sharp pecks struck more rapidly than the rapid spacer on his electric typewriter, or intermittently, like a loud, irregular escapement. On the lawn there were trees laden with ripe apples that no one picked and that fell "to bruise themselves an exit for themselves." The grounds of the college were extensive—the nearest house was at least a thousand feet away. Beyond the lawn, to the south, he walked into a field of corn much taller than he was. Soon he was quite hidden, felt himself disappearing from view, becoming invisible to any observer. Not that there were any observers—of his species. It was good to hide in freedom, as in a wood.

In the distance, almost on every side, were mountains, their outlines like great wings aslant, the open wings of a seagull. It was rather pitiful that he should make the comparison—he missed his village by the sea where his home and family were.

He returned inside to have a cup of coffee in the kitchen, and heard the cricket. How tirelessly it went on, and for what purpose? Was it simply *joie de vivre*, a song of summer, a song of summer dying? Or was it a love song, played to a mate who wasn't there, a lonely call that one might come and join it?

He sipped his coffee—instant, with a little milk—in the bare kitchen, so distant from the one at home, where there were two of his children's paintings, a Russian icon, a bronze relief of crabs over the stove, a copper pitcher from Arabia, many pots and pans on display; where his wife made Italian coffee, and where people kept dropping in— they lived right in the center of the village. Here, apart from the sink, the stove, the refrigerator, the table and two chairs, there was almost nothing, and no one. Yes, someone—he heard a door on the ground floor being opened and steps coming his way. A middle-aged, slender, mild-looking, bespectacled man, with reddish hair brushed down and curling at the lobes of his ears, appeared and stopped at the threshold as if surprised to see him.

"Hello," he said to the newcomer.

"Hello," the man replied. "I thought I was alone."

"I did too."

They laughed. "Thaddeus Dolmen," the man said.

"Emilio Buti."

They shook hands.

"That's an unusual name," Emilio said.

"Yes, people don't know what nationality. It presents certain advantages," Thaddeus said in a slight, not unpleasant foreign accent.

"I won't ask you any passport questions. When did you arrive? Oops, there's one!"

"What do you teach, may I ask?"

"A prose workshop, a course on late nineteenth-century and early twentieth-century novels, and some Italian. And you?"

"History of ideas, literary criticism and theory of language."

"That sounds very intellectual."

Thaddeus pursed his lips, exhaled and tilted his head as if to brush aside the remark. "I am a structuralist and a semioticist," he said. "What novels are you doing, may I ask?"

"Controversial ones—novels that were hard to publish; *Resurrection*, because of the Czar; *Tess of the D'Urbervilles* and *Women in Love*, because of the morals of the time; *The Portrait of the Artist as a Young Man* and *Remembrance of Things Past* because they were considered underplotted."

"Interesting," Thaddeus said, then began talking rapidly about other novels that he thought were ahead of their times—novels that for the most part Emilio didn't know; English, French, Scandinavian, German, Russian, and even Italian novels—and with such enthusiasm in three cases that Emilio thought he had better write down their titles and the names of their authors. He wondered if he had ever met anyone so erudite. Thaddeus came very close as he spoke, and more than once Emilio felt a droplet of saliva landing on his face. But never mind. It was worth it. He thanked him, which only encouraged Thaddeus to say more. With considerable zeal, he dictated two other titles and spelled out the authors' names for him. Next, he recommended a book on Dante that was unknown to Emilio. He felt so ignorant. I shouldn't be teaching, he thought. I ought to be painting houses, or gardening, though I am not very good at those things either. Oh God, what is it that I do well?

Thaddeus paused for breath, and, to his relief, Emilio heard the cricket chirp. Such a familiar, simple sound.

"A cricket," he said to Thaddeus.

"Ah," Thaddeus said, and went toward the sink. He tapped the sink. Immediately the cricket stopped chirping; then, after a moment, it began again. Once more Thaddeus tapped the sink. Again there was stillness. "He stops," Thaddeus said, "then resumes. Stops and resumes. It is funny."

"Yes. Well," Emilio said, smiling, "I guess I'd better go back up to my room and do some reading."

"Oh, there is another novel you must read. This one 1910."

Dutifully Emilio took pencil and paper again while the other dictated. "Well, thank you," he said. "You've given me quite a bit of homework. I really feel very well equipped now."

"Oh, you are welcome," Thaddeus said with a discounting gesture, as if he had offered him two peanuts, then looked down at the floor at a rather large bug, and, before Emilio could say stop, Thaddeus had crushed it under his shoe.

"No!" Emilio said.

Thaddeus stepped aside, uncovered a crumpled little heap from which two long legs stuck out, flattened.

"The cricket! You killed it."

Thaddeus looked at it and shrugged his shoulders, then rubbed his shoe on the floor. "And there's another book—" he went on.

But Emilio wasn't about to listen. "No," he said, softly, and left the kitchen. As he went into his room he still had in his hand the slip of paper he had written names on. He looked at it the way one looks at a distasteful object and, tearing it to pieces, threw it into the wastepaper basket.

the sugar maples

Near the house along the drive they stood, the sugar maples, untapped sources of sweetness, to make his life less bitter, if he willed.

He remembered, as a boy, in Canada—there from Italy, by way of England, during the war—one year in early May, deep in the woods some two hundred miles north of Montreal, where spring came late and where he had gone on a summer job with the forestry department, he struck with an ax a yellow birch, not with the idea of felling it, but just to set the ax in full view rather than on the ground where he might lose it, and the tree's sap gushed out abundantly, like blood from a deep wound, though colorless, and though the birch, of course, made no lament. As the sap continued to pour out, he watched it in amazement, stilled by the sight, then pulled the ax out and wished that he could staunch the flow. The man he was with said that, like maple sap, it too was sweet and that syrup and sugar could be made from it, though it took even more boiling down.

Ever since then, from time to time he thought of the faraway tree that he had wounded, and the sap that he had spilled sometimes was lymph, sometimes the sweetest liquid. It suggested both pain—deep cuts, hospitals, and gauze—and pleasure—pancakes, breakfast tables, camp-fires. Sometimes he even thought of the birch with its gold limbs as of a woodland nymph he had violated. Then the thoughts went beyond pain, pleasure, and shame, and he saw yellow and white birches clothed in liveliest green and heard their leaves flutter in the wind. The slightest breeze— a mere breath of a breeze—was enough to stir them.

Now his thoughts were with the maples, a more staple tree. It was March in Vermont. Spring was filtering, seep-ing in like a wave in its tentative, halting, sometimes back-tracking fashion—slow up the mountains, fast along the valleys—on its long sweep from the Gulf toward the Arc-tic, penetrating into the core of living things, imparting its own motion to them. Least to man perhaps, most or soonest to crocus and snowdrops, and—in the animal king-dom—to peepers. It stirred them into a choir. Oh, what a din they made, those heralds of the spring.

Not outwardly yet, though their stems seemed heed-ful and their buds glistened, but deep within, the maples knew it too, and were affected. The sap was running. Buckets hung from the trees along the road even a quarter mile from town. One, two, three, even four buckets to a tree. What a good kind of farming, he thought. No animals to slaughter. Maples—you don't have to prune them, till them, or climb them. No tedious, poisonous insecticides or fertilizers needed. Nothing of that sort. Just a tap and a bucket.

At a hardware store he bought, for ninety-nine cents, a maple tap—a small metal, funnel-shaped device with a keel-like projection for striking with a hammer and a ring to which a bucket could be attached—and off he went home, quite happy.

Home was a four-windowed bedroom he rented in an isolated house that belonged to the college where he taught. Five other teachers had rooms there, but they stayed only two or three days. They arrived from New York on Mondays and departed Thursdays, leaving him alone for four nights. Then the house—with kitchen, living room, and garden—was his, and sometimes he cooked or lit a fire and sat in the living room by the fireplace or wandered in the garden. A long time before, when the house had been a private home, a woman lived there who was fond of wild flowers. She had transplanted many varieties of them into the garden, and they still grew—the previous April the lawn was carpeted with violets; there were trilliums and bloodroots in a copse. The garden extended nearly without demarcation into a field. It had been seeded for corn the year before, and in September it was so tall he had almost gotten lost in it. From his windows, north and south, he could see distant mountains, and west, a wooded rise. Since he missed a full view of the sunset and the ocean, he hung on the bare walls a painting he did of a fiery sunset on the sea and one of mauve clouds with streaks of gold and saffron over a line of mountains. Yet another he did of a daffodil sky just after sunset.

Dale, an elderly Vermonter, lanky and mild-mannered, came twice a week to clean the house (all except the bedrooms) in a sparkling red van, the only flashy thing about him. After a dry spell, of which he had complained, there was a storm and he asked Dale if he thought it had rained enough.

"Oh, yes, the ground got a good soak."

It pleased him to hear him say the word "soak." It was exactly the same word that the farmers in Tuscany liked to use—"*zuppata.*"

"Do you have some land here, Dale?"

"Yes, a field back of the house."

"Ah, good. Is that a sugar maple?" he asked him, pointing to a huge tree in the middle of the front yard.

"No, that's what we call a split-leaf maple. But those along the drive—that one there, and the other, and the other, all the way down to the gate—are sugar maples."

"Did they plant them along the road so it'd be easier to collect the sap with the horse carts?"

"Yes, that could be. It would make sense now, wouldn't it?"

"I was thinking of tapping one of them."

"Now's the time."

"I bought a tap downtown. How deep should I set it in?"

"Oh," he said, crossing one index finger with the other to show a little over two inches. He smiled; he seemed amused and pleased that an outsider should want to collect sap.

"And how long will the sap run?"

"A month maybe, till it warms up."

"It doesn't harm the tree, does it, to bore these holes for sap?"

"No, it don't seem to. They heal right up."

"I think maple syrup has the most wonderful flavor. There's nothing quite like it. It's unique."

"That's right. Unique."

"I hear you can make syrup out of yellow birches, too, but it must taste different."

"I've never tasted it. All plants have sap, but there's nothing like a maple. The first sap is the finest. That's called fancy, or grade A. Then, a little later in the season, there's B. But they are all good—not much difference there. Cold nights and sunny days—that's what does it. Last year was a great year. A good tree will yield a bucketful in two or three days, if the weather's right."

Again Dale reminded him of the way Tuscan farmers spoke of the olive tree. They had the same love and admiration for it that Vermonters had for maples.

With a screwdriver—he could find no gimlet in the hardware store, only drills that cost more than buying the syrup (he had in mind to make only about a pint)—he bored a hole into the nearest sugar maple, inserted the tap, hammered it in a bit, and hung to its ring with wire a large empty grapefruit-juice can stripped of its label and with its top incompletely opened so as to serve as a lid to keep the rain out. Almost immediately a drop flowed down the tap, and soon another. He left and went to his office. When he returned in the late afternoon, the can was already a quarter full. He drank some of the sap—faintly, very faintly sweet, certainly not tasteless, not like distilled water. That sap was spring, and he was drinking it—drinking spring from a source purer than the mountain springs or the brooks fed by melting snow from which, in his walks, he also drank.

Did spring really show least in man or move him least? No, the very love that in the spring, more than at any other time, he felt for nature—especially the flowers that were so beautifully made in their every tiniest detail; and the new sticky leaves, between rose and gold, issuing from the buds; and the wooded mountains, slowly turning from brown to green; and the nearer trees, gaining in their intricacy, in their hatching and crosshatching, so that the view of houses was concealed little by little—wasn't that, too, a manifestation of spring, spring in him? Surely it was. He felt one with them, a tenderness. And, not least, love for his own kind.

That month, at a college party, a woman who taught French, seeing him alone hanging around rather gloomily with a glass of wine in his hand—his sixth or seventh—had said to him, "Aren't you talking to any of these pretty girls? Look, there's one. Her name's Astrid. She's one of my students.

Her hair was the lightest brown, the color of a walnut shell, and it went down to her shoulders in ringlets. She had a bright look, enlightened eyes. Though alone when the French teacher had pointed her out, in a moment two boys approached her and the three entered into lively, merry conversation. He watched her laughing. Pretty—and unattainable, he thought. But a little later, while he was sitting on a long sofa with plenty of room to his right, unaccountably she came to sit beside him. "Who are you?" she said, cheerfully.

"Fortune's favorite child. You are sitting next to me."

She smiled. "That's a nice compliment."

"Sitting next to you I feel invisible."

"Invisible?"

"All eyes are on you."

"I don't think that's true."

"Well, if not invisible, inconspicuous, beside you. I thought I saw spring outside, but it's within."

"Say, I'm not used to this!"

"Oh, you must have scads of admirers."

"No! You are quite wrong. I have none."

"You have me. But you are 'a metaphor of Spring and Youth and Morning' while I am one of fall and age and evening."

"They have their beauty too."

"Evening and fall, but age?"

"Yes, age too. There's more time in it, and I love time."

"You are very kind."

"I'm being truthful. I know you teach here, but what do you do?"

"I sketch."

"Don't worry, then," she said. "Artists never age."

Later he walked her to her house—one of the college dorms.

"Do you want to see my room?" she said.

"Oh, it's so late."

"I have a nice room."

"I'm sure it's nice, but—"

"Come," she said.

The invitation was made with such innocence, trust, and sureness that he was baffled. He followed her up the stairs, feeling anything but invisible or inconspicuous. What was he doing? Was this accepted? A couple of girls saw him and paid no attention. She led him down a corridor that seemed twice its length to him and finally reached her door. There were plenty of conversation pieces in her bedroom, and he wasn't short of words anyway, but at last they fell silent. He touched her arm. She stood motionless, inscrutable, looking at him. "Well, I must go," he said.

"You know your way out?"

"Yes, I'll find it."

"Good night," he said, and kissed her on the cheek.

He bought a second tap, hung another can from it on the next tree on the road, and it too began dripping. Amazing—and yet so natural. In a couple of days the first can was full. In the kitchen he poured the sap into a pan, and boiled it down to a fraction of its volume—till he had only about half a cup. And this precious, straw-colored liquid—which tasted just like the one in stores, and better, he thought—he decanted into a quart bottle, which he stoppered and placed in the refrigerator.

The next day, Dale was over, and he showed it to him.

"I saw your two cans out there," Dale said, and, smiling, took the bottle, held it up level with his eyes and shook it. "Haven't boiled it down quite enough. Just a little more will do it; it's almost there."

"I'll boil the next lot down a good deal more, make it really concentrated, add it to this, and they'll average out just right."

"Yes, you can do that."

"Do you think the Indians knew about maple syrup?"

"I'm sure they did," Dale said without hesitation.

It was good to talk to Dale. He knew the lore of the land that most, if not all, had forgotten. He talked about the Indians and the first settlers as if he had witnessed their doings, with an assurance that touched him and amused him. Often, in his teaching jobs, more than with his colleagues he made friends with the maintenance people. He remembered a lab boy at N.Y.U. with whom he would go and drink beer in a Third Avenue bar, and a cleaning lady in Indiana for whom he would go to his office just in order to be there and talk to her when she appeared around midnight. And others, in almost every place he had taught—and he had taught in about a dozen. Such were his luminaries.

One batch of sap he inadvertently boiled down to the point at which it very nearly crystallized into sugar. He was left with a tacky, chewy substance, which he tasted. It seemed as good as anything he had ever set his teeth into.

This business with the maples was a welcome relief from the teaching routine. Going back home, he would invariably look into the cans, and his joy could almost be measured by the amount of sap that had accumulated. It's the only thing that gives me any pleasure, he thought.

He took a drive with a middle-aged friend and talked to her about tapping the trees.

"Poor trees," she said. "It sounds cruel."

"No, it doesn't hurt them. At least, it doesn't seem to. They heal right up during the summer. That's what Dale said, anyway."

"Who's Dale?"

"The caretaker at my house. An old Vermonter."

"He ought to know."

"Yes, and yours, my dear, if I may say so, is misplaced pity."

After three weeks he had more than a half a bottle of syrup. Then the weather turned warm, and no more sap flowed. "It's all over," Dale said.

The syrup in the bottle had some impurities—bits of bark and other matter. He went downtown for a little sieve, explained to the saleswoman what he needed it for, and picked one out. "Oh, you want to strain it for the dregs," she said.

Glad she had supplied him with the right word, he filtered the syrup through the sieve, and now it looked clear—like the kind you buy. He took a spoonful of it. In Europe they had nothing like it. It couldn't be bought, except perhaps in some gourmet shops in Paris and in London, at exorbitant prices. As a child in Italy he had never seen it used in dishes. And yet its subtle taste evoked a memory. It eluded him, though he knew it was a memory of very long ago—one that had nothing to do with all the times he had had maple syrup in the United States and Canada. "Tastes and smells you don't forget." So where had he tasted it in his childhood? And the spoon gave him the clue—in medicines, as a vehicle to disguise bitter drugs. Yes, pharmacists used it there, importing it from far away at prices that were prohibitive for grocery stores and restaurants. A vehicle for bitterness.

He took another spoonful, and pondered on his life. Here he was alone during the long weekend in his solitary house. Every weekend and much of the rest of the week, too, except when he taught and was around the heart of the campus. And he thought: Astrid—there's another kind of sweetness. And a line of Boccaccio's recurred to him: "All pleasures are trifles as compared to love." Yes, if, under cover of darkness, he could cradle her body with his, and share the air that she breathed, and bask in the warmth that they engendered, then the magical world he'd inhabit, which the crocus's petals enclose. He thought of the crocus, the tulip, and other flowers outside in the garden, closing up at night, and he a tiny creature resting in that chamber, feeling whole, safe, sheltered, comforted, protected. With her here in bed it would be like that, only better. But to hope for such bliss was to falter, was to falter and waver besides. For how could such heaven descend on earth that was already half ashes, on earth that was withered and spent? Yet, he reasoned, winged seeds land on stark rocks, land where no softness receives them—and cinders on richest of sods. But to invoke such a fate on a loved one was a sign less of love than of hate.

The thought of her worried him. He had often talked to her since that first meeting, and she looked at him with such loving eyes. She brought him flowers to his office, left some brownies in his mailbox. She wrote him notes and seemed unable to dissemble a certain slight displeasure if he had lunch with other students or if he even walked with them. If he wanted to—he was almost sure—he would be able to cradle her body with his, yes, under cover of darkness. But she was so young, so very young. Yet one of his colleagues was surprised or didn't believe him when he told her that he had never had an affair with a student here. "I've never even kissed one," he added. "Not passionately anyway. Just affectionately."

"You are so young," he said to Astrid in his office.

"I am a senior."

"You a senior. I am the senior. A senior citizen; well, though I don't exactly qualify, how many times—in stores, in restaurants—haven't I been asked? In one restaurant I went to—Denny's—there was in the menu a listing, at reduced prices, for senior citizens—55 or over; 55 or over, and according to that description, I did qualify." There, now he had just about told her his age, though he hadn't meant to, for to tell his age was against his principles. Passport dialogue. But he *had* to discourage her, had to ward her off. He hoped she had more sense than he. He didn't trust himself. Oh, God, she kept coming to his office, after classes, if she saw a light. And he would try to keep the conversation on her studies, on poetry and painting and the weather and cities and her family; but it was difficult. Only a week more and she'd graduate; she'd be gone far away and in September she would not be back. Luckily.

How so, luckily? She was so warm, so good, generous, abundant, shapely, *beauteous*. He wanted to hold her in his arms. Sometimes he did, but gently—when she left and he gave her a parting kiss, like the one in her bedroom, to which, though she had invited him again, he had never returned.

She laughed at what he'd said about senior citizens in the menu. It seemed to mean nothing to her. It slid off her, left about as much of an impression as a drop of rain on a duck's feathers. She laughed, then turned serious and stared at him, her face flushed.

"Do you know how to cook pancakes?" he said.

"Yes, why?"

"Because I have half a bottle of maple syrup from that sap I told you I was collecting. We could have pancakes, over at my house, before you leave."

"That's a grand idea. When?"

"Weekends there's no one there, and the kitchen—the whole house—is ours. Saturday? Around six?"

"Fine."

"I'll buy the mix," he said.

Saturday, around six, he was looking out his bedroom windows for her, expecting her to come walking down the drive like Little Red Riding Hood, when he heard the telephone ring.

"Do you still want to have pancakes?" she said.

"Yes, aren't you coming?"

"I'm with Jennifer; can she come too?"

"Sure."

He watched the two girls cooking one pancake after another, pouring the thin and subtle syrup, eating.

"Your maple syrup's yummy," Astrid said.

"And so are your pancakes. Just right," he said. He paused a moment. "In fact," he added slowly and in another tone, "everything is . . . as it should be."

Jennifer hummed appreciatively, but Astrid gave him a swift, knowing look.

Soon they left; he opened the refrigerator, took out a bottle of champagne that he had bought for the occasion, brought it up to his room, and poured himself one glass after another to the end.

stones aplenty

There was, at the south end of the large, level front lawn of the college, a long low stone wall which the students playfully called "The end of the world," as if there were nothing or nothing worthwhile beyond it. A rough, uncultivated slope there was, with plenty of stones and outcroppings. It dropped steeply down toward a wood and the valley below. A few miles farther was a tall green mountain, and beyond it, on the left, a range of the faint-blue color of distance.

One morning, toward the beginning of term, when I was teaching there, I saw a series of stone structures standing on the wall. They bore a vague resemblance to human figures—at least each had a head and what could be construed to be a neck, a trunk, shoulders, and even limbs. The term "rough-hewn" could hardly fit them—none of the stones had been cut; they were intact, left as nature had made them. Yet they weren't put together in an artless or haphazard way.

They defied easy definition. Statues, monuments, pilings? Whatever they were, they bespoke a practiced hand. Something primitive and at the same time astute about them—each stone placed in such a way that made sense, well balanced, sturdy, not easily blown off. Also, I could see they had been carefully chosen, and certainly, below the wall, scattered on the slope, there was a vast assortment of stones.

I asked a few students and teachers if they knew who might be their artificer, but if they noticed them at all, they had paid little or no attention to them. At any rate, they didn't seem to know. And this, of course, added to their mystery in my mind. I praised them and asked others: "Who made those wonderful stone structures on the 'end-of-the-world' wall?" But no one I approached knew, nor did my interest rouse theirs.

Then, a few days later, a pleasant young student, a freshman, a boy, from a fiction class that I was teaching, came into my office. He didn't have anything special to discuss—no paper, story, poem or essay. He said he had just come in to talk. I asked him what other courses he was taking, and he shrugged his shoulders.

"I'm just looking around," he said. "I like to ride here and there on my motorbike. Do you want to see it? It's out there." He went to the window. "There by the wall."

I got up and looked. "It's nice and light," I said.

"It takes me over all kinds of terrain. I came to Vermont because of all the country roads here. So many of them, and each one prettier than the next or last. I have a detailed map of the whole state, and I ride from place to place. Often I stop, get off and walk along the streams, and I put one stone on another and another and another till I have a kind of statue, or not altogether a statue, a pile of stones, a shape. You may have seen what I did on the 'end-of-the-world' wall."

"Did you do those?" I said, though by this time I had little doubt he must be their maker. "I've been admiring them all these last few days, ever since I first saw them. And I've been asking about them, but no one was able to tell me. I think they are wonderful. I'm sure glad to know who did them at last—that it is you."

Again I went to see the stone structures and stood a while contemplating them. Then, a day or two later, to my dismay, I found that they'd gone. I asked a gardener about them.

"Christine had them pulled down," he said. Christine was in charge of buildings and grounds. Everyone here called everyone else, even the college president, by their first names.

"Oh dear," I said. "I really liked them. It's a shame."

"I liked them too," he said.

"Why did they pull down your stones?" I asked the student the next time he came to my office.

"I don't know."

"Pulling them down was vandalism, at no risk, by the person in charge."

"I don't care," he said. "They weren't built to last, and I have plenty more on the banks of streams."

"And if a flood sweeps them away?"

"I don't mind. I do them for the doing."

"You are a real artist," I said.

He didn't even stay till the end of term. He rode away on his slight motorcycle and did not return.

Since then, by streams and river banks, I've often paused and wondered about him and his work, hoping that envious hands and sweeping floods spared some of his shapes. And still I can almost hear him saying, "It doesn't matter."

the homing pigeon

There are people who have such a nice, invigorating and cheerful way of asking you to do something for them, that you wish they would ask you
more often. They make you feel you've been invited, not ordered to do it, and they are a pleasure
to serve. It is that they have an endearing, love-
summoning power, which he sadly lacked—at
least here at home. He didn't know how to ask,
and his wife and children weren't being obliging.
He was too plaintive perhaps, hardly energy-im-
parting; or was it that they didn't love him?

"Shut up," Delia—his younger daughter—had begun to say to him each time he asked her to close the door or turn the TV down or switch a light out, and, each time, he saw his freedom. "Shut up," the little words came out like sling shots, sharp and stinging, an expression of annoyance, perhaps even of hatred, judging from the fierce look in her eyes. He was someone she could easily do without, she whose love for him he had never doubted, whose love had been his great comfort, his mainstay in the house. How she would hug him, kiss him for no particular reason. That's what he liked best, when she kissed him not good night or goodbye, but for no reason except love. And how she seemed to need him, like him to be around, cry when he left for a long journey. And when she went to sleep for the night—which was like leaving for nine hours for another world—she would ask him to take her upstairs and tell her a story, or, if as it sometimes happened, he had no story to tell or was too tired to, just to lie beside her for a little while. Telling her a story, quite often she went to sleep before the end, and then it seemed to him that the story had really accomplished its purpose, had been most successful, when it led her, tided her to sleep. Before long, he would notice her breathing—deep, regular, slow. And how she held his hand! The feel of her hand, long and thin and smooth, so different from his own, reminded him strangely of his mother's hand, of his mother who had died a few weeks before Delia was conceived. He had the extraordinary feeling that his mother was holding his hand. Yes, that was how she held it. This little thing his mother. It was uncanny. His mother had reasserted herself through her grandchild, and nothing was more precious.

Now she had joined the others in the family—his wife, his elder daughter, his little boy—at whose hands he got little affection. He felt something inside him giving way, a shrinking feeling in his midriff, and at the same time or immediately following it, a feeling of freedom that was almost exhilarating. Ha, now he would be able to go, to leave. No bond held him any longer. He had stayed on for her. But now no more. Nothing kept him. He was free. Just because of those two words "shut up"? Wasn't it just a passing childhood fit of anger, no more than a huff or pique? Even so it had never happened before; never had she spoken, looked at him that way. Perhaps it was her age—eleven and a half, going on to twelve—and a certain awareness of womanhood, the approaching of its crises, that made her irritable. If so, good God, he should ignore it, act as if nothing had happened.

But, the thing was, he didn't want to ignore it. He wanted an excuse so he could leave. Yes, this—the way she had begun to treat him—was just what he needed, the drop that made the cup flow over. It gave him more of a case, rounded it out.

He had expected his children's love to wane as they grew up, but not quite this fast, and certainly not for it to be replaced by hatred. He remembered his elder daughter, Sally, now nearly sixteen, as a baby, screaming if he so much as left the room—no, if he so much as started to walk toward the door. Why, now she often told him to his face she couldn't stand him, couldn't bear to live in the same house with him. Oh, all for such small reasons—his insisting she do the dishes or go to bed so she could get up in time to catch the school bus in the morning and avoid his having to drive her the six miles there as he so often did. He frequently thought and sometimes said to her, "I'll leave, you needn't worry. You won't have to live in the same house with me for long."

His little boy, nine, had begun already to resent him. His father was the man who made him read.

"You've turned him against reading," his wife said.

"All right, I'll stop." He felt stymied, thwarted at every turn. And, at the same time, free.

One by one they seemed all to be driving him away. His wife kept saying, "It was so peaceful when you were in Indiana." He had spent a year teaching there.

"It was peaceful for me too," he would retort.

"Hm," she would murmur.

"I could go away for longer or forever," he would say, his voice at once bitter and wistful.

They were like pebbles, she and he, whose facets, through continuous chafing, had adjusted to each other. They put up with one another more than got along. He admired her in some ways—her integrity, her taste, her devotion to the children. In politics and art she was bright and well informed. And she helped him with his work, his paintings—that is, he trusted her good judgment. But she couldn't bring herself to say anything sweet to him. The word "darling" she reserved for houses—the two- or three-hundred-year-old Cape Cod cottages in a nice setting. She would much sooner fondle a cat or dog than him. Hugs, caresses, kisses he never looked for from her any longer. She seemed incapable of them, in his respect at least. And he had grown accustomed to her denials, and now he hardly ever made any advances anymore. Still, she endured his company and showed some concern if not affection for him. But she was proud—too proud. He knew she wouldn't say a word to detain him should he go.

Only Delia hugged him and held his hand, and now she, too, had become hostile. For the first time he felt alone in the full house.

Through the living room window he looked at the side of his sailboat leaning against the house, just below the window sill. He had brought it in for the winter. It was no more than ten-feet long and so light he could lift it, one end at a time, onto his open car and carry it that way to the beach. The beach, he thought; take it to the beach of the outer shore, the surf shore, the back shore, as the old-timers called it, the Atlantic Ocean shore on this February day with the west wind blowing. He would hoist the sail from this outermost point, head east, on his boat that couldn't sail close to the wind.

Oh, once out, there would be no return, not though he changed his mind. Oh, he would get there, there was no doubt he'd get there, to his father and his mother, there was no doubt about it. He'd see them very soon; he would see them directly. It was the fastest way. Not in months or weeks, not even in a day—in a few hours he'd see them and meet them and embrace them, they who'd been waiting for him. Open-armed and kissing as when he was a boy and came back across the ocean on a much larger boat. Oh, there was no doubt they'd be there, welcoming and feasting by the open hearth. The kindling sparkled, crackled; the flames burst out enveloping the logs, lit up their faces orange, set everything aglow. The shadows danced and wavered; the smoke hung low on the hood. Oh, would it be the same there? It would be just the same. The family reunion, the lambent flames, the embers. Then only red-flecked ashes—it was time to go to bed. Oh, he would find them on the cold ocean floor. The biting winds would waft him, would speed him, see him there. Oh yes, one had two homes: not just that of the family one husbanded and fathered, but another—that of the family one came from, dead and yet undying.

He left the window. What was the matter with him? How could he entertain such thoughts, give himself up to such vagaries, he with a wife and children to support, he who ought to have ahead of him still some fruitful years? No boat. Forget the boat. Turn to the living, to the now, the present, and not death. Freedom. What was freedom? Freedom was one's conscience. Could he get into his car and in good conscience leave? Hardly, and certainly not in the car, the only car they had. They'd had two, but he had junked the old one. "I wouldn't put any more money into it," a mechanic had told him, and he had taken his advice. His wished he hadn't. There was the bus. Step in the New York bus as 7:25 in the morning and go to the cheap, central, old hotel he usually went to for never more than a night or two. "When are you going to stay a little longer," the desk clerk had asked him the last time he was there. "I may soon," he had replied.

In New York, the girl he had again and again thought of leaving home for wasn't any longer about to receive him with wide-embracing love. He had made her wait too long, disappointed her too often. And it was ironic that, now he was ready to leave, the thought of going to live with her didn't beckon to him as it had. He didn't feel the powerful lure. He wasn't as attracted as he had been. Years had gone by—seven, eight—from the time he had first met her. What was drawing the children away from him and making him feel unwanted in his house, had also drawn him away from her, or her from him. The golden look had tarnished. He himself had weathered. His hair had thinned and grayed. He couldn't read without glasses anymore and, at alarmingly short intervals, needed stronger lenses. Sometimes it happened to him, as it had never happened since he was a child, to fall asleep in an armchair. A weariness came over him that made the staircase of the house seem almost unnegotiable. And, worst of all, a feeling that he had done his best work and that what lay ahead was only repetition. A disconsolate feeling of inertia.

In Indiana there was a graduate student, small and pretty, who had said to him before parting, "You can always come and stay with me; you know that, don't you?"

"Anytime?"

"Yes."

"Even years from now and if I present myself like a hobo?"

"Yes, always."

"You might be married."

"No."

Jenny, in Terre Haute. Why not go there? He paused to wonder. Too far. Not enough love. Wait till he was a hobo.

In Providence he knew a sculptor, built on the large scale. He could stay with her, too; she had said so. He had only to call. But he could see her large, slightly protruding eyes fixing him, staring at him with a love he couldn't match, asking, asking, expecting more of him, yet more of him. It wasn't very restful. He had been there three times, and each time—like a bird that feels the call of another land and must migrate, must fly—he had felt the urge to leave, for home. A homing pigeon.

A restful girl, one to lie next to and quite forget the past, was there such a one? Only in the past, when the past was not so heavy. Now no one could accomplish that trick for him. He went into the kitchen. His wife, with the zest that trying out a new recipe always lent her, was making kale soup. He watched her peeling potatoes, cutting carrots, severing the leaves of kale. She seemed totally absorbed in what she was doing, calm, unruffled, and with the suggestion of a smile. Later, he smelled the soup as it boiled. Then he forgot about it. It was afternoon. The sun was shining.

"I think I'll go out in the car and do some sketching," he said, a sharp pencil and a tablet in his hand. Sketching today was just an excuse, an invention, or perhaps a lie. Lies came easy to him when the truth was blunt and when telling it implied disowning kindness, which seemed the greater lie. He might yet sketch, but even if he did, that wasn't his main intention. And as a matter of fact, he didn't do any sketching; he went instead to the next town, twelve miles away, to see a girl he knew, a painter's model and a singer—not a girl anymore really, though beauty kept her young. She had an apartment overlooking the bay. He could stay there, too, indefinitely. It amazed him how many open invitations he had. He wondered why. So many lonely people. What was the answer? In his youth it had never been like this; he had never been so welcome. He went up the outside staircase to her apartment and knocked on the door. She asked who it was and he said his name and she opened the door wide and let him in and hugged him. It was good to be between her arms, to hold her between his.

the homing pigeon

Later, much later, she started cooking supper, and he remembered the kale soup his wife had made for him and for
herself and for the children, but mainly for him because
she knew he liked it best. It was her form of love now, and
dear, in a sense, as this other love, the love that he got here.
And again that urge to leave took hold of him, a restless-
ness. But he stayed on, against his will, and later, returning
home at last, he pretended that he hadn't eaten and he had
a bowl of the kale soup. From the kitchen table he looked
at the threshold. He wasn't inside the house as his wife
and children were. He was ever crossing that threshold,
ever leaving and coming back, especially in his mind.

For the children, it was time to go to bed. "Daddy, will
you take me upstairs?" Delia said. "Will you come and tell
me a story?"

"You want me to?" he said surprised.

"Yes, why?"

"No, nothing."

He went upstairs and lay beside her and told her a
story and held her by the hand. Did he say there wasn't
anyone who could make him forget the past? It wasn't so.
Lying here, beside her, his hand in hers, he was quite happy,
restful; for a moment he quite forgot the past.

company

He's on his way home for a weekend. It's a long trip—250 miles—and the first part over mountains. Often there's fog, or ice. In the five years he's been taking the drive he's gone off the road twice, badly denting his car, the first time in the fog, against a post; the second time, in frozen rain, against a railing, when even the police cars were skidding. Sometimes he wonders why he goes home at all. Not that he goes very often. Maybe once a month. He teaches art at a college and lives alone in a campus apartment. His wife refused to go and live there. Their house is by the sea. The college is in the mountains. "Too cold," she said, and he didn't insist that she move. In some ways he needs to be alone. It seems to him they've been separating for years, gradually living more and more on their own. After their three children were born, one by one they displaced him, and he took to sleeping alone. Her visits to his bedroom became rarer and rarer, till, some ten years ago, they stopped altogether. Now the children are away from home for long periods—the two younger ones at college, the older one working, all in New York. But they go home once in a while. By telephone, letter and visits they all keep in touch. They are a family yet, not split.

Still, he feels separate, if not separated. When he's home there's always plenty to fix—walls, furniture, plumbing. Little rest. No great comfort. Easier in the apartment. And more friends up at the college. More diversions. Movies, plays, concerts, shows, dances, dinners, drinks. Affairs. Down at the house now there's his wife and the cat. The two of them, alone. As he drives, he can almost see them—the cat on the sofa beside her, and she watching the news. "Well, she's very self-contained," he says to himself, "self-sufficient, too. Though hardly self-supporting." She hasn't had a job since he married her. "I'm busy every minute," she says if he ever complains about it. "Bills to pay, scholarship and income tax forms to fill, the house and the yard to look after. There's no end to it." Certainly, he ponders, nobody pays her, or even thanks her for the miles she sweeps; they take for granted the long miles she walks each day within her house. Miles upon miles, uncounted, unrecounted, all adding up to and labelled a life's journey—an undistinguished, unmeasurable trail. And yet more knowing than any other miles these miles that one travels in one's home, the unsung, homespun miles.

And her social life? Their house is in the center of town, off the main street, and a few people drop in from time to time. Nights she's alone. Her faithfulness—not exactly faithfulness, more like lack of enterprise—keeps him returning. It is like a bond. If she flirted, if she had lovers, he would feel freer. But she has only a cat, at her feet.

He's done the road so many times that he finds himself past certain places without his having noticed them. He's surprised to be way past the Sagamore Bridge, for instance. Such a landmark, and he can't remember crossing it. In fact, he's only about half an hour from home. It's midnight and he wonders if his wife is waiting up for him. Probably not. Probably fast asleep, so sound asleep she may not even hear him when he gets in. Only the cat will be sure to hear him, and blink and perhaps meow for food, the cat who at night is always confined to the kitchen so she won't wet the carpets, who is over twenty years old—twenty-four, his wife claims—so old anyway that each time he comes home he expects not to find her, but always does.

Finally he reaches the turn off the highway to the center of town. Town! Village, really, and this time of year—it's winter—almost uninhabited compared to summer, when the population increases six-fold. All but a few stores are boarded up. He meets no traffic and there's no one out. The church clock says 12:30. This was a whaling town and the bell still strikes the hour and half-hour as on ships of old, so that only a few people—his wife for one—can tell the time from the tolls. He learned the sequence once, but has forgotten. He turns off the main street up the short driveway to his house, and parks his car next to his wife's. Fortunately she hasn't forgotten to leave a space for him. Sometimes she reads till late, and then a light shows up in her bedroom, the master bedroom in the front of the house. But not tonight. The house is dark, except for the outside light over the kitchen door, thoughtfully left on. He takes his keys out of his pocket and looks for the right one. When she's alone she locks the door. Her courage is of the moral, not the physical, kind.

And he steps in, turns the light on, gets himself a glass of wine, and sits by the kitchen table, in a none too comfortable armchair, with his eyes fixed on the cat, whose eyes are fixed on his. He tries to outstare her, but she's in no mood to play the game and he feels in front of someone older and wiser than he. She blinks twice, then, her interest in him at an end, she turns away and walks to a bench by the window. She jumps up to it, gingerly enters a large brown paper bag that has been left there on its side, and disappears from sight. He almost smiles. Yes, she has her cute moments all right. He remembers her being chased by a small poodle and running behind a cane rake in a corner of the porch, and, safe there, looking at the nonplussed dog. And he remembers her being very concerned when any of the children wept, and even jumping on their shoulders and licking them in an effort to console them.

But her cute moments are few and far between. He remembers also with horror and distaste the times when—years ago, in her nimble days—she would come back to the house like a proud hunter, with a bird or chipmunk, or even a small rabbit hanging from her mouth and deposit them on the kitchen threshold as if they were gifts. Those darling creatures, any one of which he much preferred to the cat herself, and, given a choice, would far rather have preserved. Oh, he supposed he couldn't blame her for her nature without blaming the whole order of things—the ugly, yet perhaps inevitable, arrangement whereby "every maw the greater on the less feeds evermore." And yet why did he have to subject himself to such spectacles? Now she wasn't up to catching anything anymore. But unfortunately there were other things— unpleasantnesses of a different sort, the infirmities that waited on old age, the body becoming almost mechanical in its needs, the dreary routine of ingestion and excretion more prominent than in youth when food is more a means than an end. Such a time they had with her. Again and again he had to move the furniture, roll up the oriental carpet in the living room, carry it to the lawn, spread it, hose it and leave it in the sun, hoping to rid it of the telltale odor. "She was perfectly house-trained," his wife would say, "until that winter we rented the house and went to Italy. No one bothered to let her out or anything."

He sips from his glass of wine and sees the bag move as if by magic. Ah, yes, the cat, he thinks. "Are you going to outlive me?" he says. "Are you going to be with us forever?"

His wife, in slippers and pink robe, comes into the kitchen smiling. "Who were you talking to?" she says.

"The cat."

"Where is she?"

"In there."

"It was so funny hearing you say that."

"I don't see what's so funny."

"You, talking to the cat, in this old house, in the middle of the night."

She comes nearer and leans toward him to be kissed, brush cheeks really.

"Were you asleep?"

"I was just about to go to sleep when I heard the car. It's so quiet here you can hear every noise. The other night I thought I heard someone tapping and I called the police. Then I realized it was a branch. Only the wind."

"What did they say?"

"They didn't mind."

"Gives them something to do."

"In this out of the way place one feels almost suspended from the world. What are we doing here?"

"Well, you didn't want to live at the college."

"Oh, I don't want to go there. I'd go to Rome if anywhere."

"Rome," he says, "how could we live in Rome? What could I do? Teach where?" He sighs. "When I close my eyes I see the road coming toward me, the curb, the dividing line, lights."

"It's a long drive," she says.

The cat, as if unable to sleep, comes out of the bag and begins cleaning herself.

"You can say whatever you like about her," his wife remarks, seeing her lapping her white chest, her legs, in fact every remotest corner of herself, "but not that she isn't clean." And he must admit her chest is the purest white. Then she turns to the cat and says, "Yass, she's a clean kitty, yass," and the cat looks at her as if in acknowledgement, and goes on with her toilette like a workman who knows he's doing a good job. "Yass, yass, it's a clean kitty."

Again he stares at the cat, thoughtfully this time, not trying to outstare her. She had belonged to a friend who, eighteen years ago, rented their house. On their return, the cat decided to stay on, scared by a dog at the friend's new house. She was welcomed by the children, but not by him. Two or three times in fact he tried to return her, only to find her at the doorstep in a matter of hours. "What gets me," he says, "is we didn't even choose her. I would never have chosen her. She's not beautiful like some cats. Some cats are splendid, with fiery eyes, glowing orange, ember-like, and long, soft fur, mysterious looking. But she isn't. She's pretty ordinary."

"What's he saying about you, kitty? Yass, she is pretty too. Aren't you a pretty kitty?"

"It's not that I don't like cats. When I was a child we had a tiger cat. She would bask in the sun like a sphinx, and I'd lie next to her and dote on her. But this, this black and white thing—"

"'Thing' now he calls her. You are not a thing, are you, my kitty?"

"Mind you, my inclination is to like them. After Baudelaire, Manet, Colette, one would be a fool not to. Cats, they are contemplative, independent, proud, passionate. But she came to us spayed, altered, fixed."

"Poor little kitty."

"They certainly fixed her. She never goes near another cat, and so she hasn't caught any diseases. It may account for her longevity."

"She is wise, my kitty."

"Old and mangy-looking. Young creatures are easier to take care of. In fact, I think nature made the young as pretty as they are so their parents will be more apt to take care of them."

"She certainly needs a lot of care. Ooops, there she goes coughing up a hairball. Quick, open the door."

They get her out just in time.

"The times I've had to clean after her," she says. "In the summer it's better; then she stays out a lot."

"What misery."

"Oh well, don't make it sound worse than it is."

"How differently age affects animals and man. She's the equivalent of a hundred, and yet she can still climb and jump—nothing like a man of a hundred. I suppose it's because animals can't both be alive and helpless. I mean, they don't help one another as we do. They help their babies, not their elders. Once they get helpless they die, unless we look after them."

"I look after her. Eighteen years. First the children, and now her. Cat hair all over the place. But she'll get her fur all back in the summer, and lie out in the sun, and be happy. Yass, she will, won't you, kitty?"

"Each winter, I say to myself, 'This will be her last.' But it never is. She'll go on and on."

His wife smiles. "Sometimes she stays out all night and doesn't return in the morning, and I wonder if maybe she went to die. I've heard cats do that. They just disappear. But, each time, she returns in the afternoon, walks in as if she'd just gone out for a minute."

The cat now scratches at the door and his wife lets her in. "You just watch the great horned owl don't get you," she says to the cat. "Oh, look at her, how bent her legs are, and hardly any fur on her back at all."

"The mange?"

"No, just age, I think."

"We could send her to the Animal Rescue League, and they'll put her to sleep," he says.

"If she would only die by herself it'd be easier, but she won't make anything easy for us."

They go into the library where his wife reclines on a sofa and he sits in an armchair. The cat appears at the door, stops, looks hesitant, inquiring, then walks in, climbs onto the sofa, arches her back, stretches out and stalks forward as if to pounce on an inexistent prey. But her pouncing days are over, and she slowly crawls forward to his wife's feet, then to her knees, and finally lies down on her waist.

"No, you are too germy," she says, but lets her stay.

"I could call the Animal Rescue League tomorrow morning," he pursues. "Shall I?"

"No," she says. "With you and the children away, it helps me to have her here. Something alive. Otherwise I'm all alone. If she weren't here it'd be too lonely." She turns to the cat. "We are pretty much alike, aren't we? Two old ladies left alone. Poor soulie. Kitty. Yass. She's my kitty."

The words give him pause, and he thinks of when the wind howls and the house creaks and trembles as if it shivered in the cold, and the shadows of bare branches waving in the wind sweep across the walls, enlarged, beckoning like skeletal arms, and of her and the cat alone here. And on the other hand of himself at the college, of the hateful image of himself up there—his revels and the not so lonely nights. And he wants to narrow, bridge the gap that separates them, and he moves to the sofa and tries to lie down beside her, frightening away the cat. But, "No you don't," she says sharply, resisting him, making no room for him. Thwarted, he puts his feet back on the floor, rises, turns and lets himself drop back in the armchair. Feet down, legs straight, hands clasped in front of him, and head thrown back, he slumps in it. He listens to the silence. Meanwhile, the cat, seeing him slouched in the armchair at a safe distance, climbs back onto the sofa and goes to lie beside her, just where he had meant to be.

"Poor kitty," she says, stroking her.

"Poor husband."

"Well, you wanted it this way."

"What?"

"You know what I mean, you and all your girlfriends."

"What girlfriends?" he asks, but so faintly she doesn't reply. They reel in front of him—those he loved who didn't love him, those who loved him and he didn't love. Then he just sits and listens to the deep silence of the house. "There's nothing to be done," it says. "Nothing."

Nothing? Nothing is no solution, and he tries to find one. "Nothing now," he says to himself, "but in a few years I'll retire. Then I'll come here to stay and we'll be close again—the way old people are close."

crosscurrents

Lying in bed in the middle of the afternoon, he saw, through the skylight of his studio, the fronds of a weeping willow waving, telling him that the wind was blowing, nodding to him, beckoning him to rise and to go sailing. His boat—an old catamaran—was at the beach, fitted and ready. The tide, he knew, was coming in and would be high in about two hours. But still he lay, anchored by a sense of inertia and dejection to the bed.

A bird darted across the skylight. There was speed and height and song and freedom, all in one breast in the live sky where the wind was stirring, while in this room was stillness and confinement. And he must rise and go into the open air, unfurl his sail till it too flapped like a leaf, and put to sea. He went into the yard. The leaves of the maples fluttered. High above the roof, the fronds of the willow waved like seaweed, tempest-tossed. Was it too windy to go out in a small boat? The thought gave him pause, but he felt almost a call to go, insistent, imperative, and as if he had no choice. Oddly, he had the impression of paying out rope. But to whom? To what? To his taut nerves? To his life that wanted leeway?

Driving past the pier, he looked at the harbor master's pole for small-craft warning flags. None were flying, and soon he saw several sails out in the bay. One tall white one, beyond a sand ridge that screened its hull from view, moved across his line of vision, as smoothly as a swan. He parked his car, carried his gear to the boat, and in a few minutes had it rigged. He turned it around and began pulling it down the beach toward the water's edge, then pushed himself out into deep water, jumped on, pressed down the daggerboards, took hold of the tiller, grabbed the sheetline, and was off at a good clip in the direction of the headland that separated the bay from the open sea. Soon the beach was in the background, beyond an ever-widening stretch of blue. How good to be away from land, unreachable or nearly, suspended on the surface of the sea, where you lost almost all your weight and felt buoyant. Next to flying, what was there better?

Usually the wind was from the northwest or dead against him, which made putting out to sea difficult, especially in a catamaran, a boat that didn't point or tack well. Sometimes it was from the east, which was good for putting out but made returning difficult—more than once he had gotten stranded in a far corner of the bay. Today the wind, from the southwest, was just right for him—he could sail out and back without tacking, in a close reach out and in a broad reach in. And since the wind was so favorable, he thought, why not steer toward the open sea, beyond the long sand spit that extended finger-like from the wooded headland? South of the spit there was a little island that only showed up at low tide, whitened by foam and sea gulls. It was submerged now. Once, not so very long ago—less than a century—the island had been quite sizeable, even at high tide, and people had lived there. One could still find bricks, or the remnants of bricks. You recognized them by their color more than by their shape—the sea had blunted their edges, worn them till they looked like pebbles. He had sailed there before, but never beyond it. Today, with such a good wind, he thought he would. There'd be time—time to sail over the submerged island, time to get a feeling of the open sea, and time to get back home before dark.

He felt more alive in this shaky old boat than in the safety of his bed. Did speed, instability, danger make one more aware of life than stillness, security, safety? If so, leave the bay, which was hardly dangerous, and sail out into the open sea. Yes, leave all sluggishness behind.

He was now in the middle of the bay, the headland about a mile to the right and getting closer as he proceeded. With the fresh wind he was making good headway, not going as fast as the new catamarans that fairly hummed along, but at a good speed nevertheless, perhaps eight or nine miles an hour, the speed of a man running. Soon he was past the headland and sailing toward the end of the sandy spit. It stretched south for a distance that varied with the tide—about a mile now, he judged. It was so narrow and low, the spit, that he could see the open sea beyond it, and it looked a deeper blue. Every once in a while, a wave, cresting, made a little peak on the horizon. He was trying to sail parallel to the spit, but he couldn't quite. A flock of sea gulls, scared by his approach, lifted in unison and wheeled, to land again at a little distance. The spit tapered to a point. He wondered if he could sail past it without tacking. He pulled the sheetline to sail closer to the wind. He might just make it around the point and into the open sea without tacking. No, he was just twenty feet short of the point. To go around it he'd have to either make two tacks, which was easy enough, or he could land, pull the boat those twenty feet, board it again and sail into the open. He decided to land. In this way he could take a swim. It would be good to swim out here—you had the choice of two beaches, one calm on the bay side, the other rough on the open sea. And he wasn't the only one to have been attracted to this shore. Another sailboat, larger than his, with two sails, stood moored on the sand some five hundred feet away, on the bay side, and he could see three women walking along the shore of the open sea, toward the point. He pulled the daggerboards up and landed just about where he had planned, very near the point. He let the sail loose so it flapped in the wind, and he dragged the boat well up on the sand, for he wasn't sure what the tide was doing—it mightn't be quite high yet.

The three women came nearer. Then they stopped and paddled in the water. He looked at them wistfully, three handsome, buxom women. If he could only entwine his life with theirs, he thought. No, one didn't need speed, instability, danger, to be fully aware of life. Love was better. Love, art, contemplation posed little risk or danger, and might propel you to even greater heights. Yes, love principally. Through love, life was transmitted, had he forgotten? Those three—any one of them—could at a touch, at a glance even, enliven him. But human relations weren't his forte—he never found it easy to start a conversation with strangers—and he turned toward the sea, which wasn't so choosy, the sea that refuses no man, and immersed himself in it.

He swam out. An experience more direct and immediate than sailing. No wood or fiberglass between him and the sea. His own body the vessel. Weightless. In the womb once again, there where life began. He stopped to touch the bottom. He was only up to his chest, but the pull was tremendous. He felt the swirling current and the sand sliding from under his feet, as if he were in a swift river and not in the sea at all. Rip current, riptide, perhaps compounded by the tide turning, beginning to ebb. Except for his feet, that anchored him, he would be swept out. But his feet were in touch with land, earth—his habitat. Instinctively he waded back toward the safety of the shore, against the strong current that seemed to want to steal him from it, as though he were a prize. If at times he had thought longingly of drifting out to sea, he didn't now. The body, he felt very clearly, had a revulsion of death. In the face of death, he felt very rooted to life. Safe on land, he looked at the stretch of sea and wondered where he'd be now had he gone beyond where he could touch. Over the submerged island? Drowned? Out of breath? What strange patterns the current made, and how the wind whipped the waves! He looked for the three women.

Where were they anyway? Oh, there they were; they'd gone for a swim too, on the open-sea side. They swam close to each other, like three seals. It surprised him how far out they were. He couldn't help admire them. Strong swimmers all right. And then he heard their voices, mingled with the wind, and saw them waving. "Help! Help!" he made out. Half-drowned by the wind, the call sounded all the more urgent.

For a moment he stood undecided whether to swim or sail to their rescue. His boat was right at hand, twenty feet from the point; and there were three of them; and he was no longer young. He decided to sail, even though his first impulse was to run and swim toward them. With all his might he dragged the catamaran into the water and around the point, pushed himself off with the oar, held the tiller, pulled the sheetline and pressed the daggerboards down— all without a hitch, as if the emergency brought skill with it. The boat, though it made a slightly wider arc than he meant it to, moved in their direction, and soon had them at least covered from the open sea, to which they were obviously being drawn. He was bearing toward them fast now. A few feet from them, he let go of the sail and immediately lost speed. The three women, exhausted, grasped the hulls of the catamaran. It seemed the ideal rescue boat, just made for the occasion—though the wind could tip it, hands could not.

To get them aboard, that was the difficulty. He used the most improbable holds, as he grabbed them and pulled them and heaved them up. To rescue one of them, who seemed particularly weak, he dived in, swam under her and pulled himself up with her on his shoulders, her thighs around his neck. Fighting against the sea and gravity, he felt life—its value—as never before, and a strength, a suppleness he thought he had lost long ago.

At last, alive and breathing, they all lay on the canvas deck. He pulled the sail again, straightened the tiller and made for land. The offshore current was strong, but the wind stronger, and the huge sail was like a wing aslant that bore them to the shore.

The four of them sat on the sand recovering their breath. He looked at them. Oh, how very entwined his and their bodies had been, and their lives! One by one they had been in his arms, and he had hugged them for dear life— in such a different way from what he had envisioned when he had looked at them wistfully on shore, some thirty minutes ago. If fate had answered his wishes, how immoral it was—it cared only about the end, not the means or the way. It took things literally, without preambles, and liked shortcuts, then laughed irony's laughter while you lay exhausted. Had he wished for kisses instead of entwinement, would he at this very moment be doing mouth-to-mouth resuscitation on them?

The three women rose and stood like a tripod, the arms of each over another's shoulders, their foreheads in touch, their eyes staring at the sand. They came nearer to him. "Thank you," they said.

He often hardly knew what to say when people thanked him. Should he say, "You are welcome . . . Oh, imagine . . . Don't mention it . . . You bet"? None of these expressions seemed right in this case. "Oh, don't thank me," he said, "you did something for me too—I was feeling kind of at loose ends today, and you gave me something to hold onto."

Osage Orange

The lecture had decidedly not gone well. It was about form, but the lecture itself had no form. And it seemed to him now, in his room at the faculty club, that his present life was formless, too. It didn't coalesce around any point. It had no nucleus, no core. It seemed ready to fall apart. And he wanted it to cohere, to cohere the way an Osage orange cohered—so tight you could hardly nick it with your fingernail. He had once picked one from a tree along the edge of a road in Indiana, and what a beauty it was. Nothing was more compact. The urge to cohere was in him—which was something—but he had nothing to cling to.

"What about your family?" he asked himself. He was married. He had three children, a house on the coast of New England. He had been away three weeks and was to be away four more, teaching, giving lectures. They felt so loose, his family ties. To test them, he picked up the telephone. Its wire seemed something that might reconnect him. He dialed his home number collect. Michael, his little boy, ten, answered. "Hi, Dad," he said, after accepting the call. "Is there any snow there?"

"Yes, about a foot."

"Here it's almost all melted."

He remembered phoning home long distance a year or two ago, and Michael had shouted so the whole house would hear him, "It's Daddy, it's Daddy. Hey, Daddy's on the phone," a response that alone was worth the call. Today conversation was a little difficult. Perhaps he wanted to return to his TV program. "Get me Mama, will you?" he said to Michael.

"Mama, Daddy's on the phone," he heard him say, and soon his wife was on the line.

"Hello."

"Ha, hello, how are you?" he asked warmly.

"I'm all right, how are you?" she replied.

How matter-of-fact her voice was, he couldn't help thinking—as if he were calling from a mile away. He was a thousand miles away, and he hadn't called in at least a week.

"Well, how are things?"

"They are all right. How are the lectures?"

"Oh, so-so. Any mail?"

"No."

"I never got those three letters you said you mailed me. Are you sure you sent them?"

"Yes, of course I'm sure. I sent them with a book. You must have thrown them away with the wrapping. Of course I sent them. Don't blame me."

Even on the telephone, he thought. He had hoped it might serve to bring him nearer, but he felt still farther away, and he wished he hadn't called. The telephone itself irked him. He looked at its little cord distrustfully. It wasn't his sort of instrument—the intermittent, interrupting ring, and the way one tended to avoid, lest they be taken for a poor connection, the silent pauses that he liked so much and were perhaps the best part of conversation. It was worse than talking in the dark, because the dark at least allowed for touch, whereas the telephone didn't let you either see or touch the other party and made him feel bereft of two of his senses.

Then she said, "I didn't know you *bought* the painting."

"Yes," he said. She was talking about a small, inexpensive painting that he had brought home just before leaving. He had bought it from a woman, a painter he knew, because he liked it but also because he liked her. In fact, after meeting her a few times, he felt committed to buy it. He had wanted to pay for it in cash, so his wife wouldn't see the cancelled check, and he had gone to her studio with a hundred-dollar bill. But she wanted a check, which, with some misgiving, he wrote out for her. To his wife, he said that the painting had been given to him.

"Lies have short legs," they say in Italy, and his was soon uncovered—not through the check, however. "She came here to pick it up," his wife told him "'The painting your husband bought' was how she described it. She's going to take a picture of it for a slide. Couldn't you have chosen a different one? All those grays. I don't like it," she added. She had liked it well enough, though, when he had brought it home.

To see color in gray—that was being a painter, he thought. "I liked it," he said.

"Oh," she said, and dropped the matter. But it reminded him of a similar conversation he had gone through before, in which another painting and another woman were involved. And the repetitiousness of life, the feeling that nothing really new happened to him anymore, vexed him.

Then his wife said, "Bill is coming to dinner tomorrow night."

Her letting him know that she also had a friend, was, he knew, an indirect answer to his purchase. But he was glad to hear it. If only she had an affair, then he might feel less guilty, but she wasn't likely to, nor was Bill.

"Oh," he said to make her feel happy, and there the conversation ended. He felt spent.

For dinner that night he went to a restaurant that catered mainly to students, on a busy street near the faculty club. The waitresses were what drew him there—a German girl, in particular, who had come to America to improve her English and was due to go back home in a few months. Sometimes, before going in, he would look for her through the restaurant's large picture window, but, often, even if he didn't see her he would enter, thinking she might be in the kitchen, temporarily out of sight. He who was supposed to be thinking about Form. Yet she was form personified, so agile as she moved between the tables, always walking at a cheerful pace, as if to a tune, and smiling with such genuine pleasure when she saw him.

"This is a nice place," he had said the first time he went there. "There's life here. Not like the coffee shop across the street."

"Yes, but the owner is no good," she said.

"Why?"

"He shouts; he yells at me. He doesn't like me."

"Maybe he likes you too much."

"Oh, no," she said after a moment in which she didn't seem to have understood, and laughed and hurried away.

Sometimes she lingered at his table, leaning against a chair.

"I wish you could sit down," he said one night.

"I wish I could, too," she said, and ran, adding something about the owner "catching" her.

He didn't even know her name. He tried to avoid what he considered passport questions, and he wouldn't have known that she was German if he hadn't overheard her talking to a man at the next table; her accent was almost nonexistent. No, his conversation was made up mainly of compliments, all of which were quite sincere. Each time she came to his table, he had a new one for her: "Your presence comes to me as a blessing;" or, since she told him she had studied art history in Berlin, in praise of the pleated blouse she wore, "That's the kind of blouse that Botticelli dressed his angels in;" or, "I wish I could wait on you and not the other way around;" or, "When you left, it was as if the moon had set."

He felt self-conscious—self-conscious, and ridiculous sometimes—usually the oldest man in the place, his hair graying, talking like that to this young woman. As if he had a chance. But even if he had been younger, nothing would have come of it, he thought, and an incident from the past came to his mind. At Babington's tearoom, in Rome, when he was in his mid-twenties, how many times he had gone in, just to talk to the waitress who worked there. She was Danish, he remembered, a dreamy Ophelia, and there had been little more than an exchange of glances. Less even than now. And yet how easily some succeeded. The last time he had been to this restaurant, for instance, a student had stood with the German girl in the passage just a few feet from his table, and they had whispered to each other, their lips so close they seemed almost to touch.

Tonight, on his way to the restaurant again, he was thinking of a colleague who had made a face when he had mentioned that he ate there. "That's awful," someone else had said. But to him it was the best in town, and he would much rather go there than be invited to the most sumptuous dinner. In fact, when he was invited and he accepted, as he usually did, he swore to himself and wished he had the ability or quickness to make up a plausible excuse. Unfortunately, when he arrived at the restaurant she wasn't there. Another girl came with a menu, one with whom he had also spoken before, a girl who had a very graceful way about her, though she was quite different from the other. She didn't walk at a cheerful pace but at a quiet, slow one, and when she stood her head leaned gently sideways, like a Sienese madonna or a long-stemmed flower weary of the sun's heat. With one arm akimbo and her legs crossed so only one foot rested squarely on the floor, she stood and talked with him. She was very articulate, had studied six languages, and had a degree in botany, yet she could find no better job than this.

He spotted two of his students at nearby tables and remembered their essays. They wrote admirably. He often read in the newspapers that young people now couldn't write a sentence. He didn't agree. He felt lucky to be sipping one cup of coffee after another in such gracious company. For a moment, he felt part of it, but soon he was out again, wandering about the town, seeing solitude, his faithful companion, in his own shadow under the street lights, before returning to his room or to his office at the university.

In the office opposite his, on certain weekday mornings, there was a young woman with a melodious voice and laugh. She usually kept her door open, and he kept his open—to hear her. It was so different, her laugh, from the cackle of some people he knew, or the repressed nasal outburst, or the nervous giggle, or guffaw. No, her laugh was joy, pure, glowing. Her speaking voice, too, had an unusual richness. At his desk, he listened or waited to listen. "Most musical of women, speak again," he urged. She also reminded him of someone he had known, and loved, long ago. She laughed like that, the girl of long ago, and to hear her laugh he had taken her out, only to find that she laughed less and less when she was with him. Had he, by pointing out the beauty of her laugh, made her self-conscious, or had he just bored her? This one, too, he had taken out to supper, and she also laughed in his company less well, with less abandon, not with the pure note of joy that he had overheard.

Must he, then, be content with brief glances, with voices overheard? He recalled a passage in a novel: "I've never had anything approaching a successful love affair." It had made him smile, it was so candid. It also seemed to him that the narrator was a little proud of what she said. Sometimes he felt the same way. Successful affairs weren't for him. A middle-aged man having a successful love affair! How ridiculous. When he was young, he might have had one, but he had missed his chance, and now he was trying to make up for his lost youth and flirted with girls half, or almost half, his age. Perhaps when he got to be an old man he might find someone his own age; perhaps then he might even fall in love with his wife again, and she with him, and they might become one of those sweet old couples who die within days of each other, one out of grief for the other's passing. But not now! He was in the middle of the journey, and tired because he had come so far and had still such a long way to go.

"I've never had anything approaching a successful love affair," said the intelligent woman in the novel, and the sentence made him smile again. Perhaps it was simply that one expected too much of the other person's, and one's own, body. The body had its wisdom and didn't want to be dictated to. Yet how one tried to dictate to it. Not just one's self but magazines, books, doctors, psychologists all tried, and the mess they made! It was better not to insist, to dwell on brief bright moments, he thought, and, even as he thought this, desire overrode him, and he gave himself up to the most passionate thoughts of the German girl, and the other girl, and the other. No, passion could not be dismissed so lightly. It was the one thing that might pull his life together, the one thing around which it might cohere.

osage orange

And he surveyed his life, not for what would never be but for what was and might be again. One night emerged.

It had been no affair. It had been merely a night—not even a whole night—three or four months ago, in October or November, a week after sitting next to her at a poetry reading near his town. She was slender, with a clear expressive face framed by jet black hair cut straight above her neck. At the reading, the poems stirred her, visibly. She moved her head, her torso, and a few times she smiled or laughed or sighed. She looked young, but later someone who knew her told him—though he hadn't asked (how he hated such gratuitous information)—that she was several years older than he was. Anyway, as he sat there next to her, he experienced the strangest feeling of being linked to her; though they didn't touch, he felt as though currents were passing between them, trying to bind them. So intense was the sensation it prevented words. He searched for them in vain. It wasn't shyness—shyness was only the symptom of something deeper. He didn't speak to her that evening, but a party followed the next reading, a week later, and he went and somehow, by chance, not by design, he found himself sitting next to her on a sofa. He told her about the experience of the week before. She told him she had had the same feeling. It was impossible now not to hold her hand. At a certain point, she said, or warned him, that she was very passionate. It seemed like an invitation. He asked if she would like to go for a walk with him. They left the party. She told him it was her last night in town and that she had been renting an apartment all summer but had given it up and was staying at a friend's house.

"We could go for a drive," he said.

"No," she said. Her friend was a nurse on duty at the hospital that night, she explained, and in the apartment there was only the friend's child, asleep.

At the apartment, she offered him a drink, which he declined. She went into the bedroom and returned in a nightgown. A record played soft music. Magically she swayed in the half-darkness of the living room. Magically she came toward him. Later, in the extreme moment of passion, she gave a cry that seemed to him to fill not just the room and house but the whole town, and to go out like a wave against the waves of the sea that bathed the town, and to the sky.

It echoed, that cry of joy, through the months that passed; it seemed to reach into eternity, even as it had reached into the universe. It would not die. It was a cry, he thought, "such as made the world in the beginning," primeval, belonging to no time and to all time. He had seen her again, very briefly, for a few minutes in New York. She was going away for the winter, south, to the Caribbean, to work in a hotel shop, but in the spring she would be back. "And we could go to Italy together," she said. "Seriously, we could. Think about it."

He thought about it. Sometimes he thought about it. But it wasn't like thinking of that cry. No, rather, thinking of going with her brought up all sorts of problems, worries that would stay with him throughout the journey, if they ever undertook it. And—apart from the problems and worries, were he able to brush them aside for a moment— could he ever be as happy with her as he had been that night? Could that experience ever be renewed in all its wonder? Or did it depend on newness, on their being almost strangers, on its having been her last night in town—on conditions or circumstances that could not be repeated? Perhaps not. Perhaps he could be happy with her. "Go with her, then," he told himself. "Go on! Why don't you?"

He remembered posing himself a similar question when he was in his early twenties, soon after the war. He was sitting on the garden wall of his home in Italy, and a woman was sitting next to him—an American correspondent for a news magazine. She had come by jeep with a friend, a man a good deal older, a professor, a clever fellow

osage orange

whom his family had known for years. The man had left them alone in the garden. She and the man no doubt were, or had been, lovers, but now she seemed to prefer him. She was very pretty, he recalled, with bright dark eyes and an oval face, and bangs. Her hair blew in the wind. Her skirt, too. And she looked at him with a wistful eye. At one point, she said, "Why don't you come with me to Florence?" Just like that. Yes, she was all set to leave the other man, leave him cold, without a word, and take off with him. And why hadn't he gone? Why hadn't he? What kept him?

And what throughout his school years had kept him going to classes every day, to the odious lessons, the gym periods, the military drill? Why had he attended them all so dutifully? Why hadn't he followed his heart, his inclination, instead of doing what was expected of him? It seemed to him now that that was all he had ever done. Only once, in those days, did he remember doing what his heart told him: it was snowing, and he just forgot to go to school. The snow, the rarity of a snowfall in his town, the wonder of it, had made him literally forget that there was school, and he had gone into the park instead, and played, and only become aware that he was missing school when it had become too late to go.

Tomorrow he had another lecture. He felt as if he were a student all over again. That he was giving the lectures instead of hearing them didn't really matter. The strain was greater, if anything, and the students sometimes seemed to him like professors, whom he had to please, stern judges sitting there without a word. In the end, they would write a report about him: Course or Teacher Evaluation, they called it. A few students had dropped the course, dropped him, already given their judgment. He wondered what they all said to each other, what they wrote home, about him. "Good"? "No good"? What did they say? Some looked at him with a kindly eye, tenderly. But even they probably sensed the strain, sensed his difficulties. And he wished he could cut loose, give up, go away. But he couldn't, any more than when he was a student. To truly change, one had to fall into a state of oblivion. He had managed it once, during a snowfall. But here it snowed again and again, throughout the winter, sometimes even in the fall and in the spring. He had got used to snow.

reflection

Beauty, he thought, as he looked at the back of the head and hair of the girl who was sitting in front of him in the train, is an absolute. He didn't really know what an absolute was—something whose value couldn't be questioned? That existed in and by itself? Infinite? Whatever it was, *there* it was. The seats, of medium height and separate, like armchairs, all looked forward, so that he could only see the back of her head and her hair, abundant, rich, chestnut-brown, fulgent. But it was a world to revel in. Its sheen, its grain, its waves. Single hairs stood free, rebellious, in long curved lines, master strokes of a fine pencil. It was just as well the seats were arranged this way. If she were facing him, he'd have to steal glances and, were he to get caught, it might be embarrassing for her, even annoying, whereas this way he could watch her without being seen, to his heart's content. He had seen her in full when she had come into the car, past his seat, which, being next to the door, was single, and had gone on to her own—an assigned, reserved seat like all the rest in this first-class, *grande-vitesse* train between Marseilles and Paris. She had turned to sit down and, still standing, smiled to him, or at least it seemed to him as if she smiled—oh, the slightest smile, perhaps just a pleasant, courteous look, an acknowledgment of his presence—while he unforgivably, remained impassive, and she *was* beautiful, with delicate, soft curves and with her friendly fleeting eyes that had rested on him only for a moment. Everything about her felicitously expressed. And young. In her twenties. Much less than half, perhaps only a third his age.

That he was so much older was no reason for not admiring her. But he could almost hear his wife, who had preferred to remain in New England, exaggerating his years, "You, sixty-five," and his replying, "I'm not trying to marry her or anything! I have no ulterior motives," and his wife saying, "Oh." And he remembered asking one of his daughters, sitting on his right at a funeral service in their village church, if she knew who the girl in front of them was, a girl with a magnificent shock of red hair that quite took his mind off the funeral oration, and his daughter replying, "You fool," in the sternest whisper. Why? Why should one ignore beauty at whatever age, of whatever age, and anywhere, anytime, even at a funeral service? Beauty, like passion, had a "golden purity," and a painter—he was a painter—or anyone for that matter, had a perfect right to feast his eyes on it, quite irrespective of its age. It might be an old person or a child, but more likely, especially for a painter, it would be a woman in the flower of her years. He had turned to his other daughter, sitting on his left, and asked her, and she had thought nothing of it and immediately told him who the girl was. The funeral, oddly enough, and perhaps that was the connection in his train of thought, was for a boy who had died in a riding accident, and who also had long, beautiful hair, blond. His curls, which had blown and fluttered in the air, now lay matted in the tomb.

This pretty passenger wore a light pearl gray dress. He could see, between the seats, some of its pleats and folds, and they too intrigued him. An elderly man, perhaps younger than he, had come to sit next to her. The two talked a while, in French, and he caught a few words. Then she reclined and probably fell asleep.

He had seen beautiful sights on his two-week trip—dawn over the Atlantic, Paris, Rome, the Ionian Sea, Florence, Genoa, the Riviera—but this, he felt, meant more, incomparably. A person gently breathing; a gently beating heart; a being with all the intricacies of the human psyche, at rest, in front of him, two feet away. Much more meaningful than works of art or trees or crimson clouds or flashing seas or skylarks. A nearer, more intimate kinship, far more knowing, though he didn't know her. Better perhaps that he didn't know her. Better perhaps that she remain a stranger. Any information might feed his curiosity, but not nourish his wonder. He became more and more aware of her. Secretly he felt he knew her, in some undisclosed, indeterminate way. Not certainly in any I've-seen-you-before or you-remind-me-of-someone or I-know-your-background kind of sense.

Oh, he had to admit, till now this trip hadn't been exactly jolly, hardly a vacation. Tiring, without laughs, and full of the things that will happen to old, forgetful, absent-minded people. Ten days ago, on a train, well out of Rome and speeding south, he had felt in his pants pocket for his bank book—a savings one that anyone could draw from—and it wasn't there. In quick succession he searched all

reflection

his other pockets for it, and opened and ransacked his suitcases, without finding it. Had someone stolen it? Had he left it in his hotel room? When, at a station where he changed trains, he was finally able to make a call to the hotel, the clerk told him that it had been found and that they would keep it for him till his return to Rome. "*Stia tranquillo,*" the clerk said, and with a broad smile he experienced the pitiful pleasure of reassurance. Then, in Otranto in the blazing heat, while waiting for a bus in an outdoor café, he left his new light cotton jacket on a chair and only noticed it was missing when on the bus, miles out of Otranto. But there wasn't much in it, just some change. And then, though he'd read about it, he got caught in a railroad strike so it took him two days to get back to Rome. He spent the first night in a squalid hotel in a dreary town. He remembered the distances he had to carry his luggage and his left arm and hand tingling from a pinched nerve throughout his journey.

No, apart from now, there had only been two moments he could recall with any pleasure. The first had been in Boston, at the travel agency, where the agent, a visibly pregnant woman with a clear, calm, unruffled face, had been so nice and helpful to him that, when she wished him a pleasant journey, he replied that he doubted any part of it could match his meeting her. "Oh, no!" she had said, perhaps vaguely foreseeing this happy time.

Another bright moment was in southern Italy, on one of the various buses he had taken to return to Rome during the strike, when he overheard a girl talking in a lilting voice. At first he couldn't tell what language she was speaking, then it occurred to him that it was English, with an extraordinary Scottish accent. The sweetest intonations threading the rumble of the bus. A girl from the Highlands, down here in this parched, sun-bleached country they were crossing. Her words brought a smile to his face, a gloom-penetrating ray of sunlight. This was peacetime surely—if one heard the Scottish accent in Apulia. At this very same time girls from Apulia were probably crossing Scotland in a bus.

Till now only two moments. At the last hotel where he had spent the night, in Genoa, going around the corner of a corridor, the maid, meeting him, jumped with fright. Am I such a sight, he thought, and looked at himself in a wall mirror. "No, you are all right," he said to himself. Mercifully it was one of those rare, true, kind mirrors without the errors of refraction that, no matter how slight, can quite spoil your looks. Marseilles had been so disappointing he had spent most of his time in a café. After an exasperatingly long wait at the ticket booth, he had barely made this train, hopped on it just as it was about to leave, aided by a good-natured conductor who waived some slight irregularity about his reservation with the words, "Bon, bon." And now he was here, where he wanted to be. There was no other place he'd rather be in.

The train was fairly speeding across the Midi. At what? 175, 200 miles an hour? The electric power poles along the railroad, spaced at intervals of at least 300 feet, went by in rapid succession, one after the other, at the rate of seconds in a clock. The names of the small stations the train didn't stop at were unreadable for the speed.

As the hours passed and the light of the sun changed, her reflection in the window, blurred at first, asserted itself and became more and more distinct. Soon he could see her well, and from her hair his eyes slipped to the reflection of her face and paused there. Beautiful beyond measure her image, seeming to penetrate the glass and go beyond it to veil the meadows and the woods, and then the night. He rested his eyes on her eyes, her pouting lips, the delicate curves of forehead, cheek and chin, her hair again, in front, and the side he hadn't seen. Some strands spread over her brow, hiding part of it most artfully. It was bliss to look at her unseen.

If he could only speak to her, have some communion with her, have her. Have her? But now? In what way? In

reflection

his own way, of course. Quickly he picked a pencil and a small piece of paper out of his pocket and, holding it on his address book, he drew her reflection—she was resting her face on her closed hand, her fingers beneath her orbit, a wonderful pose—and in a few bold strokes he had her. Had her, had her likeness, had her beauty, captured her, at the first try. He was so pleased with this little drawing that he stopped looking at her and looked at it instead. He didn't have to look at her anymore—he had her there. He wanted to show it to her, give it to her, for wouldn't that be a wonderful excuse to speak to her? But no, he wanted to keep her, have her. If he gave it to her he'd lose her. It wasn't even a reflection—only the drawing of a reflection, but her reflection, *her*. The train was nearing Paris. Carefully he put the drawing in his address book, closed it, put it in his pocket, and immediately had the feeling he had picked a violet to squash it in the pages of a book, or, worse, captured a butterfly and pinned it down. The pleasure was all gone. How evanescent pleasure was, elusive as a spirit, peculiar, almost perverse. He took the address book out of his pocket, the drawing out of the book, and, as she was about to leave, he leaned over to her and in his halting French said, "*Mademoiselle, je vous ai dessinée. Vôtre image sur la fenêtre. Peut-être qu'il ne vous déplairait pas de l'avoir. Je voudrais vous le donner.*" (Mademoiselle, I've made a drawing of you, of your reflection on the window. Perhaps you won't mind having it. I'd like to give it to you.) And, as she looked surprised and a little hesitant, he added, "*Je suis peintre.*" (I'm a painter.)

"*Ah, c'est très bien, merci, monsieur,*" she said, accepting it and looking at it brightly, with a smile.

And there it was, pleasure, flying again, its wings restored. As he watched her going down the platform of the Gare de Lyon with his drawing, for a moment he felt he was with her.

fall and rise

One afternoon in May Nell got a call from Edith, her solitary elder sister. In the middle of the night before, in her stocking feet, she had slipped and fallen on her bedroom floor and could not get up. Her left leg hurt from the hip down. She couldn't move it. Finally she had dragged herself to the telephone.

"We'll come right away," Nell said, "but it will take us two hours to get there. Shouldn't you call 911 and get an ambulance?"

"I'd rather not. I can wait."

Nell spoke to her husband, Lorenzo, then they hurried to get ready for the long drive into Boston.

Edith lived alone in a fourth-floor studio walk-up near a small bookshop she had once owned with Dale, a soft-spoken and quite enterprising African American, some ten years older than she. The two had been far more than business partners, but though he had no children and was more or less estranged from his wife, he never managed to go and live with Edith. They had met in the late fifties when she worked in a large downtown bookstore and he ran a janitorial service. For years he lived in a townhouse which he held onto bravely before giving it up to real-estate developers who had bought all the other houses on the block. Age, illness on his part, and his moving to the suburbs, dampened their relationship. His visits to her became rarer and rarer till he stopped seeing her altogether.

Though after that she never spoke of him to Nell and to Lorenzo, and though they had stopped asking her about him, they knew she still felt devoted to him and to African-American causes in general. In fact it was hard to talk to her about civil rights without her assuming a distant, slightly condescending tone, answering their questions with studied delay or falling silent altogether, as if to let them know that she was far more aware of the problems of African Americans than they could possibly be, having, through Dale, been thoroughly involved in them, seen them first-hand. Several times, in their bookshop, blacks had walked off with books under her own eyes, but she never had the heart to stop them. They caught on to this and began taking advantage of her. When he took a more forceful attitude, she retired to her tiny apartment, only occasionally going to the store, and limiting herself to ordering books and doing other paperwork at home.

It was six or seven years now that the bookshop had been sold. She saw practically no one. One by one her friends—she had never had more than a few—disappeared from her life. Little by little she stopped phoning her relatives and family, even Nell who was the closest to her. Besides Nell, she had another sister and an older brother, both married and with children and grandchildren. Nell would at long intervals give her a call to hear how she was doing or to invite her for Thanksgiving or Christmas, or in the summer to ask her to come and stay awhile, each time offering to drive her over, since taking a bus seemed too much of an effort for her. In the past she had accepted the invitations, but more recently she would answer in a small voice that she was all right and decline to come. A brief conversation would follow, nothing like the old ones. Years before, when she was still seeing Dale, she would call Nell quite often, confide in her, and be on the phone an hour or more, till Nell would finally tell her she had to hang up, when there'd be a long silence and then a muted goodbye.

"She can't get over him," Lorenzo said to Nell.

"I wish she would."

"Oh, I don't know; of all the pains love causes none is worse than the recognition that it's over."

She became a recluse, almost agoraphobic, going out only for bare necessities—to a nearby supermarket, the post office or the bank. She spent her time reading or watching TV on her minuscule set, staying up late into the night. She was very thin and frail, but intense and proud, fierce too and resentful should anyone even inadvertently ask the wrong question or say a word she might construe as critical of her. Undemonstrative, ineffusive, she kept her distance and seemed quite self-sufficient.

Everything in her life had become smaller. Years ago, before moving to her present walk-up, she had lived in an apartment with a living room, a bedroom, a good-sized kitchen. Now this postcard-size TV set seemed to define her state. But she said that if what she saw interested her she forgot size, things became vast, measureless.

Nell would worry about her, and so would Lorenzo.

"Why don't you give Edith a call?" he'd tell her.

"Why doesn't she ever call *me?*"

"Go on, call her; you haven't called her in months."

"All right," she'd say, and put it off. Like Edith, she too was a proud person and didn't see why she should always be the one to initiate calls and extend invitations.

Finally in her own time she'd phone. "Oh, I called Edith," she'd say, days later.

"How is she?"

"She's all right."

Strange, Lorenzo thought, this slackening of ties. He remembered Nell saying that Edith was not just her favorite sister, but her closest friend. Selfless, kind, fair.

Two or three years ago, listening to the news, Nell and Lorenzo heard there'd been a gas explosion from a broken main on Edith's street. Nell immediately called her, but there was no answer. She called the police then. They said that the telephone line had been severed by the explosion, but that her sister and her building were all right.

"God, if something should happen to her, how would I ever know?" Nell said to Lorenzo. "There's no one she's in touch with."

"It must be the case with a lot of people. Now there's not even the milkman anymore . . ."

"At least when one is married . . ."

The incident made her concerned and apprehensive. To Lorenzo it seemed that only something going amiss brought people to their senses.

One day, shortly before she fell, the phone rang and he answered it.

"Robert," a voice said, indistinctly.

"Who?"

"Robert, Robert," and he gave his last name. It was Nell's brother who hadn't called in two or three years.

"Oh, Robert, how are you?"

There was a moment of silence, then he said, "Sheila . . ." Sheila was his wife.

"Wait," Lorenzo quietly said, "I'll get Nell."

She was in the kitchen. "It's your brother," he said. "I think there's something wrong."

Nell hurried to the phone. Sheila had died, of a heart attack, that morning.

At the cemetery, where Nell and Lorenzo went with Edith, Robert and his two daughters, Lorenzo barely recognized the middle sister, Jane, and her children, now grown up. Nell and Jane hadn't met since their father died, twenty years before. They kissed. There were a few friends of Sheila, and some old cronies of Robert, who would go to his funeral or he to theirs, depending on who died first. There had been hard feelings between Nell and Jane, whom Nell considered very selfish, especially with regard to their mother, long since dead. But now everything seemed well. Death brought people together. It had the power to reconcile and mend. After the funeral, at Robert's home, an hour away, one of his daughters, Sally, brought out a photo album with a picture of Edith taken during the war when she was a Wave, about to board a train to Washington. She was smiling brightly, looked full of hope and expectation, and Jane, who was in the picture too, looked lovely, quite unlike the white-haired woman with tinted glasses at the funeral.

It was only a few days later that Edith slipped and fell, and now Nell and Lorenzo were on their way to her. They reached Boston, phoned her rental office, and with the superintendent leading the way, opened the door to her apartment, and found her on the floor, patiently waiting. Lorenzo, whose father and grandmother, in Italy, had broken their hips, immediately suspected that she had fractured hers, and said that it was imperative for her to go to a hospital right away. She looked at him vaguely like a wounded thing, and with a sigh acquiesced. Nell called a well-known hospital nearby for an ambulance. In a few minutes, looking out the window, Lorenzo saw its red lights flashing down the street, and he went down to meet it. With

fall and rise

extreme ease—she barely weighed a hundred pounds—two orderlies picked her up, set her in a special chair and carried her to the ambulance. Nell rode with her, and Lorenzo followed by car.

So from solitude she was driven to the world of doctors, nurses and technicians, a highly active, densely peopled world. The health care system of the city, state and country came to help. And it was beautiful, this service. Intensive care, where human skill is put to its best use, was given to her. Modern medicine took her in hand, showed what it could do. She had never been in a hospital before; now she was part of it—the patient, on which all the rest turned, suspended between health and sickness, the focus of attention, of a concerted effort. If you weren't involved in it, health care was something you continuously heard about from a certain distance, now she was brought into its orbit, face to face.

A fracture of the hip was diagnosed, and Lorenzo thought of his father and grandmother who, in their early eighties, untreated or poorly treated, had languished, till a year or two later they had died. He felt that here things would be different, for sure.

He and Nell didn't see Edith till after the operation the next day. A metal screw had been inserted, holding together the severed bone. They met the young orthopedic surgeon. He was confident the leg would heal. "She's got a lot of spunk," he said.

In a day or two she was sitting in a wheelchair. After a few more days she was sent to a rehabilitation center. Nell and Lorenzo went to see her during visiting hours one afternoon and happened to find Robert and Sally there. Edith was in a wheelchair on a terrace in the sun and they were sitting near her. They were very quiet and seemed quite sad.

"This is nothing like being sick with a chronic disease that gets worse and worse," Lorenzo said to break the gloom. "This is a healing process—the cells silently dividing and subdividing to form new bone. It's quite wonderful really."

"Wonderful?" Edith, still in some pain, said. It didn't seem so wonderful to her, but she knew what he meant and nodded.

"Yes, wonderful," Lorenzo asserted cheerfully, and Robert, who seemed so heavy-laden and mournful, showed a flicker of a smile.

From the rehabilitation center near Boston, she was sent, after a week, to one near where Nell and Lorenzo lived. Each time they went to see her she had stories to tell of other patients there. She made friends with a number of them, and with the nurses and the doctors, and got to know some of the gossip, which she gleefully related. "I'm hardly alone a minute," she said.

In their car they drove her to the city for a checkup visit with the orthopedic surgeon, who took more X rays and was satisfied. "She's doing very nicely," he said. "Yes, making good progress." He showed them the X rays in her presence. Lorenzo looked at them. There was her pelvis, there the femur, its head and neck, the hip joint, and, a very distinct shadow, the metal bracing the bone. He felt he was seeing more than a naked picture, and wondered if she, so private, minded. On leaving, she thanked the doctor with unaccustomed fervor.

She moved from the rehabilitation center to their home, into Lorenzo's studio, which was on the ground floor. Social workers came, and every afternoon a nurse to give her exercises and to look after her. They heard Edith talking away heartily, volubly, as she never talked to them. "She gets along a lot better with her than with us," Lorenzo whispered to Nell.

She had dispensed with the wheelchair at the second rehabilitation center. Here she got around with a cumbersome walker, which soon was discarded for a four-pronged aluminum stick, then with a simple and quite elegant cane, and at this point the visiting nurse stopped coming.

fall and rise

She went nimbly about the house and even into the yard, and then across the street to a store. It was a little like seeing a fledgling learning how to fly. As time went on, more and more often she did without the cane.

"It's quite extraordinary how well you walk," Lorenzo said. "It's by far the best thing that's happened this whole summer."

But now that she was well or almost well, the question came: where would she go to live.

"Not back to your fourth-floor walk-up," Nell said.

She had applied for a low-rent apartment in a housing complex for the elderly in a nearby town where many years ago her family had owned a summer cottage by the ocean, but there was a long waiting list.

She was used to having a home of her own, to being independent, and it was difficult for her at the house, where she was all too aware that Lorenzo had been put out of his studio. He missed it. Nell often was tired and showed it. Fall was in the air. Its first chills came.

"I think I should go back to my apartment in Boston," Edith said, and Lorenzo saw her resuming her old ways, becoming solitary again, a recluse, out of touch, except for her minuscule TV set.

"No," Nell said, "that's out of the question."

"Why? I could have things delivered."

"We'll find a ground-floor apartment near here."

"Here or in the city, soon," she said.

They phoned the housing complex only to be told that she might have to wait till spring or even a year. But then, quite unexpectedly, in December, she received a letter from its manager saying that she was at the top of the list. Soon an apartment became available. She could move in on January 7th.

They drove over to see it. The housing complex—87 apartments in various buildings—was like a village within the town, in a wooded area, a mile away from the cottage her parents had owned. The apartment itself, on the ground floor, had been freshly painted. It had a living room and a bedroom, a well-equipped kitchen and a bathroom with handrails, a telephone and two emergency push-buttons. The windows looked on the village courtyard on one side, on a wood on the other. A very pleasant woman who lived on the second floor showed up and welcomed her. She was the housemother. A little bus made the rounds of town each day. In a central building was a large common room with two landscape paintings that Lorenzo much admired. They had been done by a woman who was a tenant there. And there was a piano and many books. Edith went into the adjacent manager's office and signed a check for the first month's rent.

"Well, that seemed just right, perfect," Lorenzo said, in the car.

"Yes." She looked very pleased, and even proud now she had paid the rent and it was her own.

"Isn't this known as a model town?"

"Yes," Nell said.

"No wonder. We should celebrate," Lorenzo said, and they drove to a restaurant where Edith ordered a highball to start with.

"Isn't it strange that it's so near your family's cottage on the sea?"

"Yes."

"And wasn't it you who chose it?"

"Me and my father."

"It's as if fate or the hand of chance guided you here. Your slipping and falling and hurting yourself was hard, but, as Shakespeare says, 'There is some soul of goodness in things evil.'"

doves

On a beautiful afternoon last June, I went, as I often do, to the harbor of the seaside town I live in, and sat on the thick, square wooden beam bordering the pier. Opposite me, about thirty feet away, two pigeons—their iridescent plumage glorious in the sun—stood facing each other with their beaks joined as in a kiss, and, never letting go, bowed several times to one another, all the way down to the beam. Five or six times in succession they did this, their beaks ever in touch, as if the kiss must last and they depended on it.

Then she stood still and crouched while he hopped behind her and, lifted by the slightest motion of his wings, lay on her back. The union lasted no more than a few seconds, but in that time, hidden by the softness of their plumes, in momentary darkness, the fluid of love and life was duly transmitted.

Outside, boats weighed anchor or unfurled their sails, trucks and cars rumbled in the distance, but none of all that bustle meant or mattered nearly as much as the doves' stillness where life's secret unfolded.

Then they paused. She looked a little ruffled by the experience, but soon recomposed herself. Inadvertently I lifted an arm and they flew off in a wide upward spiral that spelled freedom and took them out of sight.

It was no more than a few weeks before I too flew away, but on stiff wings, in a crowded plane, across the Atlantic Ocean, to Italy.

Seated in front of me was a young couple who, from the way they kissed each other again and again, immediately reminded me of the doves I'd seen.

A talkative, humorous man rose from the seat next to mine, and leaning over toward them, noticed they were wearing wedding rings, and asked them if they were on their honeymoon. They nodded and laughed.

Later, they rose and I was able to see them in profile. He, tall and with an arm around her, and she, snuggling close to him, had the serenity of nuptial figures in Egyptian sculpture—a bright look, directed not so much at the objects in front of them as at the future that they had in mind. Again they kissed, their lips sealed for a long moment and letting go only to kiss once more, as if their desire could never be sated. They looked at each other and smiled with predilection.

Except for the two doves, I had never seen such a loving couple. They seemed quite unaware that anyone was observing them, completely absorbed in each other as they were and quite oblivious of the world outside. They weren't showing off; there was nothing exhibitionistic about them, as with couples I have seen at dinner parties who, with a rather too obvious display of affection, flaunt their intimacy, ignoring everyone else around the table. No, here the subdued light half-hid the two, and the tall backs of their seats screened them, giving them a certain privacy. But the space between the seats was sufficient for me to gain a fairly good view of their heads, for they often turned toward each other and were in touch, her head softly resting on his or on his shoulder; and again and again they kissed each other's hair, mouth, cheeks, temples. Oh, kisses without number. . . .

Sitting as I was behind them, I couldn't help but see their hair—his a lustrous brown, so thick and abundant it made you want to pass your fingers through it, comblike. Little wonder she often grazed it with her lips. Hers, though not quite as remarkable, seemed also inviting to the touch— a wealth of resilient, blondish curls bobbing over her forehead, ears and lovely neck. They surely doted on each other. It was love undeniable and uncloyed. And I wondered, how long can such a love last? Would they be as close to each other on their way back as they were now? I was inclined to doubt it.

But two weeks later, as I was waiting in line to board a plane for my return flight to America, playful chance brought us back together. There they were, ahead of me, making their way toward the gate, he in shorts and with a knapsack and she close at his side. And again, every few steps, they leaned toward each other for a kiss, just as lovingly as before. Yes, their love was no less steadfast. It hadn't faded any, nor, I was sure, had that of the doves. The couple didn't sit anywhere near me this time, and I lost sight of them for the rest of the trip.

A few days after I got home, I went down to the pier and looked for the doves, but I didn't see them, or any others. It was full summer, and who knows where they were now; perhaps they had flown to other, cooler climates, to the north.

Thoughts of love and birth, and of the north, led my mind to wander to a small town in the Berkshires I had stopped at on my way to Vermont, where I used to teach some years ago. There, in a gift shop, I had bought some postcards and semiprecious stones from a young woman, visibly pregnant, like Botticelli's Spring, standing behind the counter. Before leaving, I asked her for directions to a gallery of arts and crafts that I had read about in the town. She told me to go to the end of the street and that I would see it on my right.

"How far is it?" I said.

"It's near."

"Like how far?"

"This far," she said, laughing and bringing her open hands close but not quite in touch with one another.

How sweet, I thought, to tell me the distance that way and not in feet, yards, or tedious fractions of a mile.

I was so struck by her graceful way that the next time I drove through that town some months later, I made a point of stopping at the shop. And there she was, behind the counter, with a baby in her arm, who was the baby she had been expecting and was born.

"What a beautiful baby," I said, after buying a few things.

She smiled. "Say, 'hi,'" she said.

"I don't suppose you remember me, but I came here some months ago, before the baby was born. It really is lovely to see you both," I said and made toward the door.

Again she laughed. "Say 'Bye,'" she said.

And the baby gave me a broad and radiant, memorable smile, then, bashful hid his face in his mother's arm.

So the story ends, but what do its parts have in common? Oh, love, of course, and, as always, time, and the cycles of the moon. But principally time. It is the great connector, though often more subtle than a thread.